AT THE EDGE OF THE WOODS

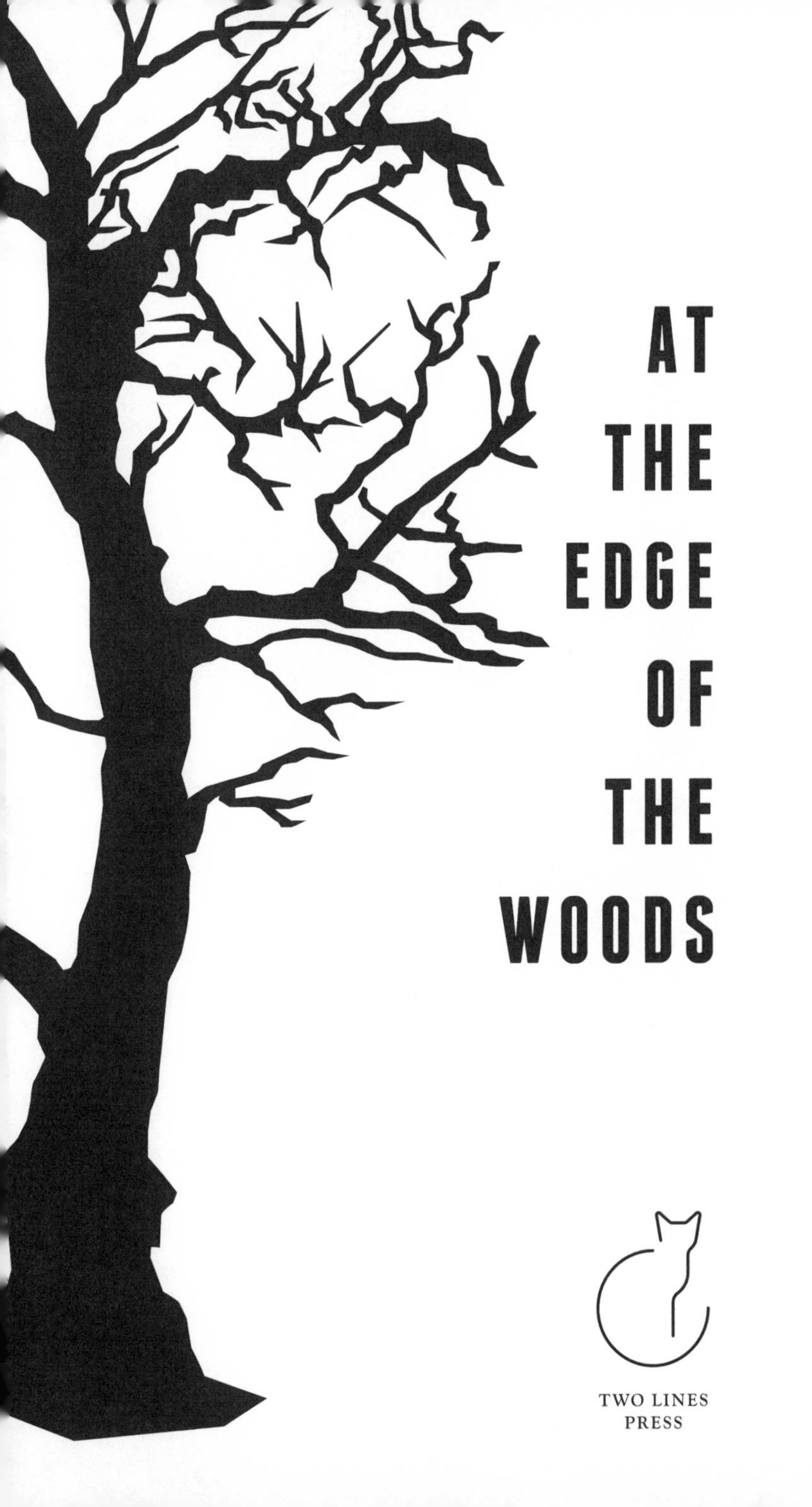

AT THE EDGE OF THE WOODS

TWO LINES PRESS

ALSO BY MASATSUGU ONO
FROM TWO LINES PRESS

Echo on the Bay
Lion Cross Point

Originally published as: *Mori no hazure de*
by Bungeishunju Ltd., Japan

"A Breast" and "The Cake Shop in the Woods" were first published in English in the Keshiki Series by Strangers Press at the University of East Anglia, through UEA Consulting Ltd.

Two Lines Press | www.twolinespress.com

ISBN: 978-1-949641-28-8
Ebook ISBN: 978-1-949641-29-5

Cover design by Kapo Ng
Design by Sloane | Samuel

Library of Congress Cataloging-in-Publication Data:

Names: Ono, Masatsugu, 1970- author. | Carpenter, Juliet Winters, translator. Title: At the edge of the woods / Masatsugu Ono; translated by Juliet Winters Carpenter. Other titles: Mori no hazure de. English Description: San Francisco, CA: Two Lines Press, 2022. | Originally published as: Mori no hazure de by Bungeishunju Ltd., Japan. | Summary: "A psychological tale of myth and fantasy, societal alienation, climate catastrophe, and the fear, paranoia, and violence of contemporary life" --Provided by publisher. Identifiers: LCCN 2021036650 (print) | LCCN 2021036651 (ebook) ISBN 9781949641288 (trade paperback) | ISBN 9781949641295 (ebook) Subjects: LCGFT: Novels. Classification: LCC PL874.N64 M6713 2022 (print) | LCC PL874.N64 (ebook) | DDC 895.63/6--dc23
LC record available at https://lccn.loc.gov/2021036650
LC ebook record available at https://lccn.loc.gov/2021036651

3 5 7 9 10 8 6 4 2

This book is supported in part by an award from the National Endowment for the Arts.

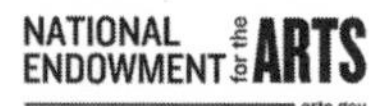

A BREAST

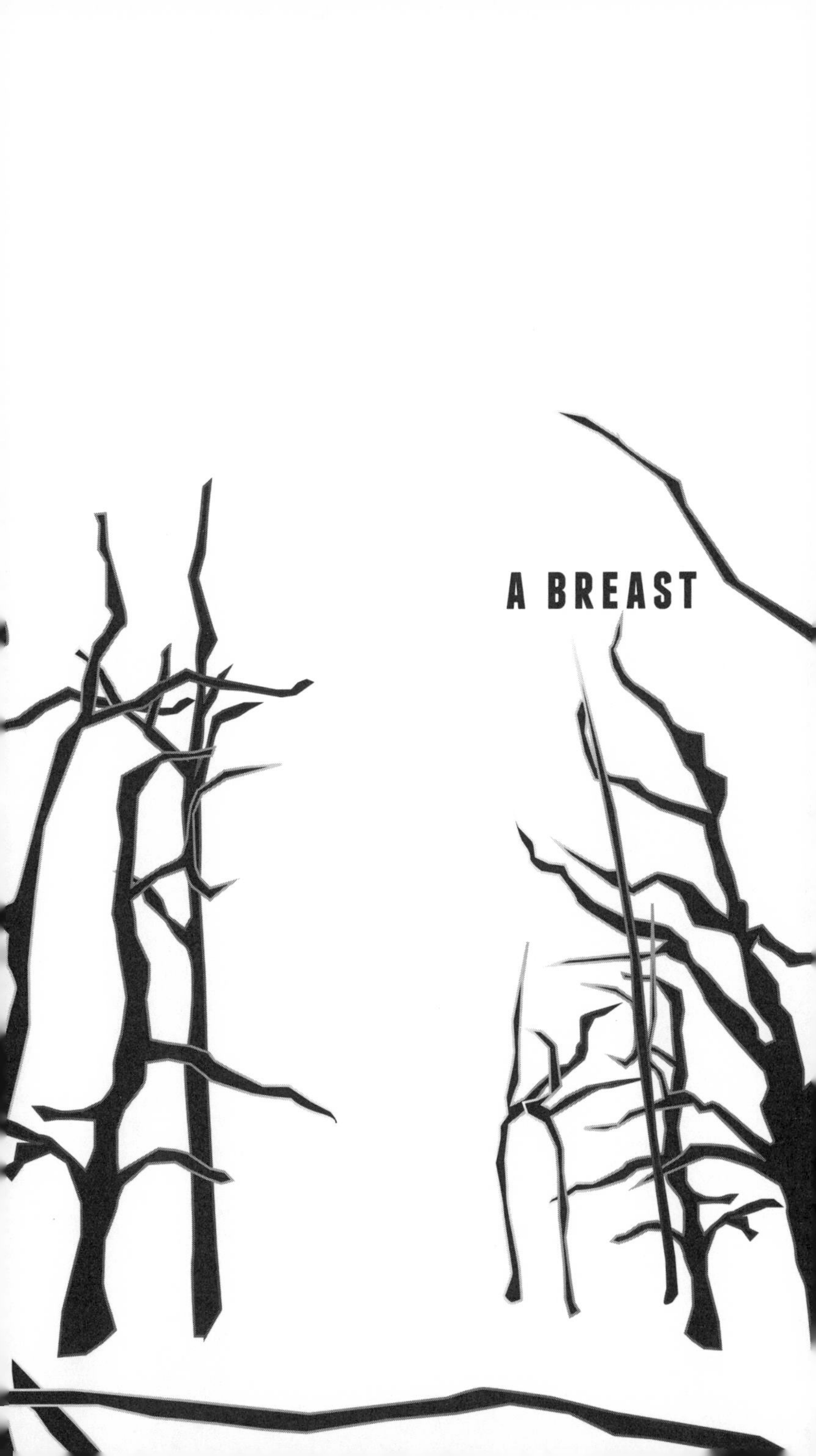

My wife had gone back to her parents' home to have our second child, leaving me and my son to manage by ourselves for a while. He's a talkative boy, we had radio and TV, and the house didn't seem particularly quiet with her gone. The reverse, in fact–extra sounds began to mingle between us.

The sounds seemed to be coming from the small woods behind our house. In truth, I don't really know whether the woods are big or small. You can't tell anything from just the map. I have the feeling that they're small, that's all.

We would go into the woods. Then a copse of trees closely resembling one another would follow us and pass us by. The trees would pat each other familiarly on the shoulders and back and sometimes wriggle their hips as they hurried on ahead. They huddled their green leaves together, absorbed in whispering, paying us no mind. Their whispers spread through the woods like the sound of distant waves. As they traveled, the whispers blotted out not only gaps in consciousness but also the interstices between trees, between branches. Unable to penetrate into the depths of the woods, we would come to a standstill.

But we weren't the only ones left behind. The trees, too, would stand transfixed, their roots tangled in fatigue and loneliness. Under the ground, loneliness joined loneliness; a vast desolation filled the woods. Though it was daytime, as if groping for light from the depths of blackness the trees stretched their leafless branches skyward. Our white breath was no substitute for lost leaves. We'd turn and go back the way we came.

Once we knew that my wife was pregnant with our second child, early every evening the three of us would walk for the better part of an hour through the woods. While we walked, she would talk continuously, addressing the unborn child. But it wasn't only her voice that drowned out the whispers drifting through the woods. The boy would repeat his mother's words, mimicking them exactly.

He kept his eyes averted from her swollen belly. He walked looking down and now and then, as if struck by an idea, kicked up some fallen leaves.

At this rough gesture, the whole woods would sharply draw in its breath.

When he was tired out from walking, he'd get crabby. Monotonous whispers in the woods would begin again to fill everything. They stole across the back of his neck and into his ears. They beckoned him to sleep.

"We have to walk a lot for Mommy and the baby in her tummy," I would tell my son, who would be rubbing his eyes as he walked. My words only made him crabbier. He'd look at me resentfully. I had no choice but to pick him up.

"When you were in Mommy's tummy," my wife would say, finally talking to him, "we used to walk a lot, too."

But he couldn't hear her. By then he'd be asleep in my arms, his mouth moving.

I would strain my ears to hear.

The murmur in the woods steadily deepened.

That sound came back. My son and I went outside. We entered the woods, careful not to rustle the carpet of leaves.

I stopped. He looked up at me, scarcely breathing. "Think it's a fox?" he asked. "Or a badger? Maybe a squirrel?"

"One thing's for sure," I said, widening my eyes. "It's not a bear."

He realized this was a joke and put both hands over his mouth to keep from laughing. I did exactly the same thing, shrugging. His shoulders rocked with happiness. Fragments of suppressed laughter spilled from between his fingers.

Leaves were falling, even though none of the branches around us had any leaves left to shed. I thought this was highly peculiar, but decided not to tell my son.

Because he wouldn't understand? Or because I had no explanation to give him?

I put my hands behind my ears, the fingers aligned and pointing straight up, searching for a sound that I could not yet hear but that I sensed was lurking somewhere very close by.

"A rabbit!" My son imitated my pose.

Then from the darkening sky leaves fell without cease, like mutterings of broken words which, apart from their rejection of meaning, made no attempt to commune. For the most part they were drawn to fallen comrades lying dead on the ground. Some, perhaps unaware that from the moment they left the branch they themselves were dead, took their time falling, scrabbling at the air. Those leaves, due to the weight of the air they scraped away, might make a sound when they struck the ground.

My son was watching me dubiously. Right. I shared his opinion.

"No," I said, "it's not the sound of falling leaves, is it."

We stood there in the woods a while, waiting, but the sound didn't come back.

"What time is it?" he suddenly asked.

I shook my head. I wasn't wearing a watch.

"TV show?" I asked.

He nodded. We walked back to the house, hand in hand. I opened the kitchen door, and he ran into the living room.

I looked at the clock on the wall and turned on the radio. Checking the program guide, I saw it was time for a special Janáček concert. The String Quartet no. 1, *Kreutzer Sonata*, had just ended, and the piano piece *In the Mists* was starting up. I turned up the volume and prepared to wash several days' worth of dishes piled in the sink. The instant I twisted the faucet handle, a stream of cold water flowed into my body. I had trouble breathing. I rinsed the dishes over and over again.

My son was sunk into the sofa, watching his show. His mouth kept moving, as if he were feverish.

I picked up a picture book from the floor and sat down beside him. I opened the book on my lap. An owl twisted its head from the page and stared at me. Although its beak was as tightly shut as its eyes were wide, a hoot flashed through me, a glimmer of light. Startled, I turned and looked behind me. Backed by darkness, the window-pane showed the living room. Only my son and I were in the frame.

Engrossed in the television, he was oblivious to my presence beside him.

The sound reverberated. From eleven at night until two in the morning, it was especially noticeable. When I got out of bed, I picked up the book I'd been reading from the floor where I'd dropped it. Normally my wife put our son to bed in his room, but while she was away he was sleeping with me. The lights were on because if the room was pitch dark, he said he couldn't sleep. What kept me awake, however, was the sound.

Light bestows sleep: I think those are the words of the German Swiss writer Robert Walser. Whereas vast, powerful darkness awakens us. The inviolability of darkness makes us want to enter deep inside it, he said. Darkness shakes us, kindles desires we never knew we had.

Standing by the window, I opened the book in my hand. In the encroaching darkness the letters filling the page formed an ever finer mesh, warding me off. The sound grew louder, harsher. The mesh on the white page shook. It rose and fell and stretched taut, as if to bounce back any fresh occurrences of the sound. Something captured and confined there was seeking to emerge. More was rent by that sound than the night that embraced our helpless selves.

Then, for the first time, I thought I knew what the sound was. No wonder it made my heart ache. It was the sound someone makes who's sick at heart. A sound like coughing. A rope tied unevenly in knots, trying to strangle you from the inside. Escape is impossible. Countless hands grip the ends of the rope and never give up. Whenever the hands menace, drive them away by coughing, that's all you can do.

The sound that came from the woods, piercing the night, was trying to strangle my heart, too. I knew it was echoing in the dreams of my son, asleep in the same bed. Every time the sound came, his small body couldn't help wriggling under the sheets like a segment of earthworm.

I looked out the window. The apple tree, the lone tree in the yard, was heavy with fruit. On the ground beneath it lay fallen apples, under attack by starlings scattering screeches as if scraping impure metal; the wounds on the fruit were the color of rust. Those remaining unfallen turned red all over, as if to say how annoyed they were with themselves for having let slip their chance to set off, and they kept on swelling, weighing down the branches more heavily each day. *You need to prop those branches up*, I'd been telling myself.

But that night I was in for a surprise. The branch I'd thought at greatest risk of breaking already had two props, like an exhausted king with two faithful retainers supporting him by the shoulders so he could manage to stand. Who could have done it?

Since the time my son and I began to live by ourselves at the edge of the woods, various strange things had been happening. *The Origin of Species*, which I was reading before bed, alternating with the *Confessions of St. Augustine*, disappeared. It should've been where I left it on the bedside table. Where could it have gone? I wondered if my wife might have put it somewhere, and I asked her about it when I called.

"You know I'd never read that," she said. And then, as if she found the notion hilarious, shrill laughter poured out of the receiver. I had to smile.

My son had gotten up and now stood beside me.

Rubbing his eyes with one hand, he clenched my pajama bottoms with the other.

"Did you do it?" I asked him.

"Do what?" he answered sleepily.

I picked him up. "See that apple tree? See the props under the branch there? Did you do that for Daddy?"

"No."

"No, I suppose not," I said, still holding him.

"I can't sleep," he said, his arms wrapped around my neck.

"Why, because of the sound?"

Before I heard him answer, I felt his warm, comfortable breath tickling the back of my neck. All at once the apple tree beyond the window shook violently. The props beneath the branch seemed about to slide out. The branch would break and the tree would topple over. Invisible wind shook it even harder. I held my breath, listening in the depths of my son's quiet breathing for the sound of falling apples.

Like the breathing of a sleeping child, the hills gently rose and fell. The dark woods turned into a nightmare, encroaching on the orchards and pasturelands scattered on the hillsides. I drove the car amid that quiet breathing. Every time I came to the top of a slope, the view opened up before me. Village after village appeared, only to then be swallowed in the waves and quickly disappear.

I was on my way to the shopping center. Open

twenty-four hours, the giant shopping center rose like a castle before my eyes. The road went uphill all the way.

From the parking lot, which was so big that it could easily have held a couple of soccer fields, you could take in the surrounding scenery far into the distance. It felt like being king of the world. In that sense, too, the place was castlelike. To go shopping at a place so high up, you really had to have a car. What were people who couldn't drive supposed to do? Vassals unable to drive need not apply, eh? Or was this the message: "Let those who can drive help those unable to get around"? Were they trying to get each person to come to grips with his own morality?

From this modern castle, the true castle couldn't be seen. I knew there was a building called a "castle" in the depths of the woods we lived beside. It was the former residence of the feudal lords who ruled this area several centuries ago. It's possible that the coughing from the woods was the echo of sounds made there long ago. Sounds of cannon fire to repel enemy troops who aimed to seize control of the land. Perhaps the woods trembled at the unexpected revival of memories of that sound, searing physical memories.

Whether the old woman came from the castle or not, I couldn't say.

When I asked my son, who returned from the woods hand in hand with her, all he did was shake his head.

"You don't know?" I kept my voice low so she

couldn't hear, bringing my face close to his. "But you're the one who brought her here!"

"No, I dunnooo!" he wailed.

He wasn't the only one in tears. The old woman, seated in a kitchen chair, stared with moist, unfocused eyes at the cup of tea I'd made for her.

He was to come home before dark, and he was not to go too deep inside the woods; under those two conditions, I allowed him to play by the woods. The trees were sparse at the edge of the woods, so from the kitchen window I could watch him kick up dead leaves along with his soccer ball. That eased my mind, which was my mistake.

Mistake? What could be mistaken about my son bringing home an old woman?

But she wouldn't stop crying, so I'd become concerned that perhaps there had been some mistake.

When I saw him leading her by the hand, I couldn't hide my confusion. She was wearing a long white garment like a bathrobe, but the sash was untied, the front open. She wasn't wearing anything underneath. And since her left arm wasn't in the sleeve, her left breast showed. It hung like an empty leather bag, and from the tip drooped a black nipple like a clot of blood. Neither blood nor milk came from that dried-out breast. Tears, however, fell from her eyes.

My son looked up worriedly at the old woman's face. From time to time she patted his head. The breast swung. My son's soft hair was thoroughly mussed.

"Thanks, dear," she said to him over and over.

Not just her skin but her voice, too, was dry. Was it because all the moisture in her body had spilled out in the unceasing tears? Her voice seemed cracked; perhaps that was because I'd noticed she was trembling. I looked away from her pubic hair, which was shining as if wet.

"Go on," I said. "Drink it while it's hot. Warm yourself."

She nodded. Lifted the cup to her lips and sipped the tea. From her pale neck down to the top of her breast, her skin seemed to flush a little.

"Is it good?" my son asked shyly.

"Yes, dear, thanks." She laid a hand on his head. "Thanks always for everything, dear."

Always? My son's expression brightened when he heard the word.

I began to understand.

Both my parents and my wife's parents were still living. But because they lived far away, our son saw his grandparents once or twice a year at most. Many of his friends lived with their grandparents, and when he went to someone's house to play, he came home captivated by having been in the presence of a gentle grandpa or grandma.

He was especially fond of the grandmother of the little girl who was his closest friend. The old woman returned his affection, often taking him shopping, making him tarts, or gathering mushrooms with him. He told us all about what he did with her, so absorbed in the story that he'd forget to eat his dinner. He chattered on like one possessed, till I wondered if he might have eaten a weird mushroom. Joy and excitement rolled around on his tongue instead of food.

When my wife ran into the little girl's mother at the shopping center, she thanked her, and the sharp retort was: "Nicer to strangers than to her own family, she is." Mothers- and daughters-in-law never seem to get along.

Anyway, for a while our son begged his mother for a grandmother and wouldn't take no for an answer.

"You already have a grandmother and a grandfather," I said. "Two of each, in fact! You can have your pick."

"Nooo," he whined, near tears. "I want a grandma that's all mine!" He kept this up, tugging on my wife's skirt.

"They *are* yours, silly. Daddy's mother and Mommy's mother, both." My voice was loud.

"No, they're not." He looked at me.

"Yes, they are. You just don't get it, do you!"

"No need to get so hot under the collar," said my wife.

"They're not!" he cried. "They're not all mine!"

"Why not?" I asked.

"'Cause they're not." He pouted. "'Cause they'll be my brother or sister's grandmas, too." He patted my wife's burgeoning belly as gently as if it were marked FRAGILE.

Later, recalling the incident with my wife, I marveled at how children come up with ideas that would never occur to an adult.

"Don't worry," she said, sipping herbal tea. "When I

was little, I went through a stage where I insisted I wanted a penis. My poor parents."

"A penis?"

"Yes, I thought department stores sold everything." She sighed, and then laughed suddenly. "Even penises!"

"But what floor would they be on?"

"Gosh, who knows. Anyway, I was sure a department store would have them." She was trying to stifle her laughter. The teacup in her hand swayed, and tea spilled onto the table. She didn't seem to notice.

"They don't sell grandmas anywhere," I complained. "They're not pets."

She wasn't listening to me. She was laughing. She sounded as if she were trying to copy the sound of her own laughter.

My son wanted a grandma all his own to dote on him. In other words, he set out to make a pet of someone who would make a pet of him. That was the only explanation for what he'd done.

My wife and I might have been the cause of this whole thing. We would break hard, stale bread into tiny pieces and scatter them from the kitchen door. We didn't do it to attract birds. We just thought that rather than throw the bread away, it would be better to feed it to them.

Thrushes began coming quite close. Sometimes if we left the door open, one would hop right into the kitchen, watching us as we sat chatting at the kitchen table. One brown female was especially brave.

My wife would put a finger to her lips, signaling to the boy to sit still and not make a sound. Our time would stop. The thrush would wag her tail with a trembling motion, moving time forward. She would hop all the way under the highchair to pick up a bit of cold cereal our son had dropped. Then she would try to pick up another piece, but since the first one kept her beak open, this didn't go well. She would tilt her head in all directions and poke at the second bit, but she could never quite manage to pick it up. Hungry chicks were waiting for her. *Pipi, pipi, pipi.* We could hear them calling her in the distance. Easy does it. Oh no! The first bit fell out of her beak; now she had to start all over. We exchanged glances, trying not to laugh, but sounds escaped us. We moved. Quick as a flash, the thrush beat her wings and flew outside.

"Must be good for birds, too, huh?" our son asked, looking up at his mother. "'Cause it's organic, right?" Jordans Organic Morning Crisp, which my wife bought at the store, was a favorite of his.

"Right." She smiled.

"That bird might taste good, too," I said. "Like organic chicken." They ignored me.

We went outside. We could see a pair of chicks, tail feathers twitching as they begged for food. *Pipi, pipi*: their cries flew through the air and were sucked into the woods. I felt as if I, too, were being begged for food. The mother bird carried food to their open mouths without a moment's rest.

"They're bigger than she is," said our son, in a tone implying that his case was different. "Big babies, that's what they are."

My wife and I looked at each other and laughed. Our son realized we were laughing at him and scowled at his mother. Seeing his sulky face, she laughed even harder.

We threw breadcrumbs to the thrush mother and her chicks. Our son was thrilled. Day by day the birds lost their wariness and came closer. This seemed to give him great satisfaction.

The mother bird had the nerve to come hunting for food in the kitchen even when we weren't there. Not just the floor but the tabletop and even the stove would be soiled with little reddish-brown droppings like crushed cherry pits. We started having to close the door when we left the kitchen.

It was around then that our son began saying he wanted a grandma all his own.

When she finished her tea, the old woman began to talk, wiping away her tears. From time to time there was the sound of someone trampling dry leaves. Someone could have been outside, listening to her story.

"I wanted a child," she said. "It was back when the country was occupied. My husband was in the demilitarized zone. I went to see him. Walking, of course."

I looked at my son. Realizing that my eyes were on him, he shook his head firmly.

From the woods came the sound of coughing. The interval between coughs was smaller than usual. He looked out the window, holding his breath.

"The railway tracks had been blown up by bombs. There was a temporary ferry next to the bombed-out bridge. Every boat was packed with people and their belongings. When I got off the ferry, I walked some more. I walked twenty-five miles a day. Fortunately I had on a pair of wool socks. When I found a stream, I'd take off my socks and wash my feet. All I really did was soak them in the cold water."

There was the sound of coughing. The old woman began to squeeze her exposed left breast, wringing it as if it were a cloth, in evident pain. My son looked away. However hard the old woman squeezed, nothing came from the dried-out breast.

"You had a terrible time," I said. My son nodded solemnly.

"My husband's unit had been disarmed, and they were in a barracks in town. He had only a two-day pass. I arrived a day early and stayed that night in an inn near the station, which was half-demolished."

"Only two days?" I asked. My son looked up at me in surprise.

"I waited for my husband at the barracks gate. He looked well. I ran to him, threw my arms around him, and pressed my lips to his. He tasted of tobacco."

I looked at my son. He looked away.

"Just a minute, please," I said. "How about another cup of tea?"

She nodded. It was hesitant, but definitely a nod. I stood up, teapot in hand. My son got off his chair and came over to me.

"It's dangerous," I said. "Out of the way." Still, he clung to my legs.

I took the kettle off the stove and poured the rest of the hot water into the teapot. The old woman's figure was reflected in the window. She was looking down, fiddling with her nipple with the tips of her fingernails. I noted that her nails were dark around the edges, as if she'd been clawing at the depths of night.

The sound of coughing went on. It sounded like someone unable to escape the rope within him, trying to end his life. How many more knots will it take before the final knot, the one that ends the coughing?

I set the teapot on the table and sat down. My son pushed his chair over right next to mine and sat. He gripped my sleeve with one hand.

After a brief pause, I poured the old woman a fresh cup of tea.

"Thank you," she said.

"Not at all," I replied.

She sipped her tea and went on with her story:

"I said to my husband, 'I want a child. Your child.'"

I nodded. That was all I could do. My son tugged hard on my sleeve, his eyes riveted on the old woman.

"'What are you talking about?' he said. He seemed really upset. 'There's a war going on. I could die anytime. How could I do something so irresponsible?' I shouted at him, 'I know!' I tugged him and pushed him with all my might down into a clump of grass by the side of the road. 'But I want a child! Your child!' I said it in a loud voice, clutching him."

I sipped my tea. My son, watching me, held out his hand. He didn't like tea, but I handed him the cup anyway. He slurped some. Then, making a face, as if he'd tasted something nasty, he handed it back.

"I had only one night to spend with my husband. If I let it go by, I would never have his child. It was a very quiet night. I straddled him and cried out loudly, flinging myself around; then in the darkness I saw it. The steel body of the locomotive stopped at the station platform was darker than the night. It never budged. But it made a sound. Struck by the core of the night, it rang with a high-pitched sound: *kin, kin, kin.* Our lovemaking was fierce. The sound struck us. And we made a baby. My son."

Overcome, the old woman buried her face in her hands. She trembled violently, and a sob escaped her. I looked up. The kitchen windows were all closed. And yet in the air there hovered the sour smell of decayed leaves from deep in the woods, leaves that would never dry out. Steam rose around the old woman. The steam was not from her tea.

"Oh!" my son cried out.

A puddle was forming at the old woman's feet. He covered his nose and mouth with both hands.

I went to the bathroom and filled the bathtub with hot water. I put some detergent in a bucket, grabbed a cleaning rag, and went back to the kitchen. My son was standing a little distance from the old woman. He was clutching a table leg and staring spellbound at the expanse of urine that had spread like melted wax, sparkling in the light.

I put my arm around the old woman's shoulders and led her into the bathroom. I took off the wet, yellow-stained robe stuck to her bottom and tossed it in the washing machine. Then, after rinsing her off in the shower, I poured a generous amount of liquid soap in my hand, worked it into a lather, and placed my hand between her legs. I moved my fingertips carefully and washed her clean. She gave no resistance. She was standing perfectly still, one hand on my shoulder.

"Can you finish washing yourself in the tub?" I asked.

She nodded, looking vaguely abashed.

While she bathed, I mopped the kitchen floor and cleaned up the excrement on the chair. It was considerably more work than cleaning up thrush droppings. I thought I heard the sound of coughing now and then from the woods, but that was the least of my problems.

When the cleaning was done, I changed my clothes. Then I knelt in front of my son and looked into his eyes. "When the old lady finishes her bath," I said, "tell her to put on the bathrobe hanging on the bathroom door. Okay?"

"Where are you going?" he asked.

"To the store." I stuck my wallet in my pants pocket. "To buy diapers."

"Nooo," he wailed. "Don't leave me, Daddy. I wanna go too."

"Come on, you know we can't leave her here all alone."

"But..."

"She's your grandma, isn't she?" I said in a strong tone.

His head dropped, and he went silent.

"If anything happens, call me right away on my cellphone."

With that, I got in the car and drove through the hills to the shopping center.

As I was tossing two packs of adult diapers into the back seat of the car, it finally struck me that something was wrong. What had I been thinking, leaving my son alone with that strange old woman? Did I do it because I'd convinced myself that she really was his grandma? As if now that he'd claimed her for his own, she would stay with us permanently in our house?

I called home from the parking lot.

The line was busy. He might be talking to his mother. If so, that was a relief. It meant he was all right. I redialed the number several times on the way home, but the line remained busy.

I turned on the car radio. Someone was reading aloud the ups and downs of the stock market in a monotonous drone. I quickly changed the station. Strains of Offenbach's *La belle Hélène* came on the air. It was just at the point where everyone was urging Helen's husband, Menelaus, to go to Crete. I was not in the mood for this, but despite myself I smiled. Soon I saw the hilltop village and tossed the phone on the passenger seat.

The moment I opened the front door, I had the feeling that the sound of coughing was coming from inside the house. I heard the television from the living room. Maybe the old woman and my son were nestled comfortably on the sofa, watching TV. Like a cat and its owner.

"Where's your grandma?" I asked.

He was absorbed in the television and didn't hear me. Or possibly he could hear only his own voice, filling his mouth.

"Where's your grandma?" I asked again.

"Quiet!" he said, his face serious.

Fed up, I went over to the TV, stood in front of it, and turned it off without a word.

"Hey! What're you doing! No fair! Come on!" He was on the verge of tears.

"Grandma," I said, grabbing him by the shoulders.

"What do you mean, 'grandma'?"

To keep from frightening him, I steadied my voice. "Your grandma. The one you brought home from the woods. Where is she?"

"Oh, her," he said in a relieved tone. "She went home."

"She did?"

"Yup."

"When?"

"Um, I think when I was talking to Mommy on the phone."

"You called Mommy?"

"No, she called me. She says she's fine. She wants you to call her back."

I went into the bathroom. The tub was empty, and it and the tile floor had been scrubbed clean. The bathrobe still hung on the back of the door. I looked inside the washing machine. No sign of the white garment she'd been wearing.

In the kitchen it was the same. The cups and teapot were washed and neatly laid out to dry in the dish rack. The white porcelain of the sink shone with a smooth, caressing light. The strong smell of cleaning solution stung my nostrils.

I went back into the living room, where my son was sunk in the sofa watching TV.

"Did you and your grandma do all that?"

As if mindful of my previous impatience, he answered right away. "All what?"

“The cleaning up. Did you and she do it together?”

“I didn’t do anything. I told you, I talked to Mommy on the phone.”

“So your grandma did it all by herself?”

“What do you mean, ‘grandma’?” He looked at me stupidly.

I was dumbstruck.

The sounds emerging from the TV drew him back to the screen. His expression as he stared at it could not have been more intent. His muttering began to mingle with the sound of the TV, and like a wound closing, the world sought to regain its proper shape. There might be a place for me in that world. But I had a feeling that I would be denied entry. The one who entered would not be me. All of the sounds humming at the bottom of the space around us invaded and filled me. That was how they rejected me.

I couldn’t take the uncertainty anymore, and called my wife. I wanted to know what our son had told her. Had he even talked to her at all?

“Grandma? He never said anything like that.”

At least they did talk. That much was clear.

“No? Then what did he say? The line was busy the whole time I was gone. What were you two talking about all that time?”

“I don’t know. Was it really that long?”

“Twenty minutes, at least.”

“Maybe he left the receiver off the hook?”

"Could be. Anyway, I'm glad you called him. Thanks."

"Oh." She sounded slightly surprised. "*He* called *me*."

Still holding the receiver, I turned and looked at my son. He was lying sprawled on the sofa, still watching TV. His feet were up on the back of the sofa and his head looked about to fall off the cushion, but he appeared unaware of the position of his body. His mouth was moving. I could almost make out the sounds wriggling inside his mouth. I pressed the receiver hard against my ear.

"What's wrong?" my wife asked through the receiver. "What is it?"

"He says you called him."

"Did I?"

"You're hopeless."

"You're no better," she said. "Did you ever find *The Origin of Species*?"

"Not yet. He found his very own grandma, though..."

"Where could it have gone?"

"Don't ask me. I don't know where she came from in the first place."

She laughed. "Not her. Your book, I mean."

I hung up the phone. Then I asked my son, "You still want your own grandma?"

There was no answer. For an instant, the coughing from the night woods split the sound of the television. Perhaps I should slip outside. In the smooth windowpane without flaw or distortion, my son was alone in the living room.

THE OLD LEATHER BAG

The other line was long.

The one my wife was told to get in moved ahead smoothly, like a string being reeled in by an invisible hand.

The other line moved not at all. Its flow blocked, the line grew denser and denser, till it might have ruptured at any moment. No one was in charge. No barrier, no rope, no cordon provided order. Despite this, the packed line did not overflow and come surging over. People squeezed together, shrinking their shoulders, pressing against one another, cheek by jowl. They endured patiently.

In the old station's open ceiling, which resembled the skeleton of a giant bird with wings outstretched, the hovering murmur was a cold, clinging mist. It took my wife some time to realize that what she heard wasn't the voices of the dead trading faraway whispers, unaware that anyone was listening.

She saw a mother holding an infant, its face pressed against her breast. Bound fast in the chill of the murmur, mother and child appeared frozen. White breaths emerged from the mother's mouth, then vanished. The infant seemed to be stifling something.

Stifling what? Not crying or laughter, not a scream. Something more powerful: the joy of life. A force that welled up unbidden and unsought, engulfing a tiny being even when it was wrapped in the warm film of sleep.

But who or what was forcing the infant to stifle this? Over its head my wife saw only a face like a fatigue-cracked wall where a withered vine of hope barely hung on. What lay beyond that wall, she could not see.

Whether the agent had brusquely stamped her passport or cast a suspicious glance at her train ticket, my wife couldn't recall. Nor could she remember whether words had been spoken or what the agent had looked like—or even whether the agent had been male or female.

Now here she was, seated aboard the high-speed train that connected two countries. She reclined her window seat and looked out idly at the still-motionless scenery. Her hand held a plastic cup of coffee. She tried to sip the scalding beverage through the little hole in the lid, burned her tongue, nearly dropped the cup.

Lukewarm breath grazed her cheek.

She turned to find an elderly woman leaning over her, face close enough to make a confession she didn't want overheard, mouth working hard. My wife instinctively drew back. The woman's face took on a fleeting look of hurt; the look of someone casually informed they have bad breath.

No. That wasn't it. My wife merely couldn't understand the words she was speaking. Finally she realized the woman was saying, "The window seat is mine."

My wife's ticket was tucked into her backpack on the overhead luggage rack. Since the woman had not produced her ticket, there was no way to confirm the seat numbers. Still, my wife assumed the woman was right.

"I'm sorry," she said in the same language the woman had used and stood up. Holding the cup of coffee, she stepped out into the aisle.

The woman shoved by and slid heavily into the window seat. She was apparently uncomfortable, and fidgeted restlessly like a dog making a bed for itself. She checked the seat under her bottom. Tried to cross her legs, couldn't, gave up. The problem wasn't lack of space; rather, her legs were too fleshy. By the time she finally settled down with an elbow on the window frame and a hand propping her chin, the scenery outside the window had begun to slowly move.

My wife marveled at the woman's enormous bosom. The front of her chocolate-colored sweater was stretched tight, as if at any moment the weaving might burst and her breasts tumble out.

The sleeves of the woman's sweater were rolled up to the elbow, and a burly forearm occupied the armrest between the two seats, spilling over into my wife's space. My wife felt heated pressure from the arm. Then the woman reached into the leather handbag on her lap and pulled out a phone. She cradled it in her hand and stared at it. Her fingers proceeded to tap out a number, hesitantly, then restively, caressingly.

My wife looked away. When the woman began to speak, however, her voice was inescapable.

My wife's eyes met the narrowed, disapproving eyes of the middle-aged man across the aisle. She had no intention of defending the woman next to her, but neither did she wish to demonstrate solidarity with the man by a sigh or a meaningful roll of her eyes. She turned her head and studied the coffee cup she had placed on the tray table in front of her.

"Don't let yourself be pushed around!" the woman said forcefully into her phone. My wife stole a sidelong glance at her, piecing together the sounds of the still-alien language as best she could. The woman's eyes were wide. What did she see? Her gaze was fixed on something. What was it? Her eyeballs seemed on the point of popping out. As if to force them back in place, my wife shut her own eyes tight. Then the woman's voice came flooding into her ears.

"If Mother says something weird, set her straight immediately. Yes, that's right. That's what the doctor said, too. The most important thing is to correct any contradictions on the spot. Otherwise, she'll drift off and never be able to come back.... Who, me?"

After a moment's silence, her tone grew harsh.

"Ha! Don't be ridiculous! What do you mean? I'm

not running away. This is a vacation, okay? I've looked after her for all this time. Surely I'm allowed a break. Every once in a while, I *need* a break. I'm entitled to it!" Pause. "What? Mother said that? Really? She's still saying that? Honestly, it's always the same. She's said I've been running away from her since before I was born." Pause. "Yes, that's what I mean. The minute she says something like that, you've got to set her straight. Really, stop and think! Run away? How could I? Seriously. I was a baby. A fetus. That's right, not even born yet! How on earth was I supposed to run away from my mother's womb?"

The woman fell silent. Then her body began to tremble with increasing force, slowly, like water set to boil, until tight laughter poured out of her. The vibrations of the coach were shredded by her convulsions.

Perhaps the trembling that welled up in the woman was transferred through her shoulder, which pressed against my wife's. My wife's body responded with a slight, rapid tremor. Laughter she could not stifle escaped her lips.

Suddenly the woman's arm crossed in front of my wife. Her pudgy left hand grasped the coffee cup on the tray table. With the phone still to her ear, she raised the cup to her lips.

The woman's neck bent backward, as if someone had grabbed her roughly by the hair at the back of her head, forcing her face up. She was being made to drink something against her will.

I'm suffocating. The moment my wife took air in her mouth, it turned to sludge, blocking her trachea.

My son, lying on the living room floor reading a picture book, raised his head and looked at me. Dusk, that scout dispatched by cautious night, was up to something, whooping it up in a corner of the room.

"Where are you going?" he asked.

"The kitchen. You want something to drink?"

"No." He shook his head. "I'm not thirsty."

I left him in the living room and went into the kitchen.

The coffee maker was still on. I poured what was left into a mug and took a sip. It wasn't hot enough, and it had boiled down to a thick liquid. I added water and put the mug in the microwave to reheat. Why should I go to all this trouble just to drink lousy coffee? I emptied the mug into the sink, lowered my face to the faucet, and drank water out of the spigot.

When I returned, Night already held the greater part of the living room. I saw my son's back. He was standing by the phone, receiver in hand.

"What are you doing?" My voice was surprisingly loud, even to me.

For a moment, Night wavered.

Not only Night was taken by surprise. My son spun around with an exaggerated motion, as if an internal spring had come uncoiled, and looked at me with fear in his eyes.

I switched on the lamp on the mantel. We use

energy-efficient lightbulbs, and it takes a while for them to light up. Little by little, Night was forced back outside the windows. Bits of nocturnal darkness that failed to escape hid in panic under the toys scattered on the floor and in the curtain folds.

If the phone had rung, I would have heard it.

The boy's eyes were full of tears. They were dark and large, reflecting the light like nighttime pools of water. Why was he looking at me like that?

I had to ask the one question on my mind. "Was it Mommy?"

"Because it's tied down?" he murmured, rubbing around his eyes with the back of his hand.

"What?"

"Because it's tied down by the cord, the baby can't get out?" He looked up at me. "Is that why?"

Is that why? Why what? What should I say? How did he want me to continue this conversation?

There was a time when every day I would make up some outlandish story to tell him. He would listen with pleasure and sometimes think up what came next. The plot would develop in unexpected ways, go off on tangents, and I took pleasure in devising twists to surprise him, capturing and drawing out his curiosity. In the stories, death was a mere roadside weed; the tone was invariably cheerful and pleasant and comical, seedlike scatterings of sadness going unnoticed. But I had no memory of ever having wandered with my son into a story involving an umbilical cord. I also had to admit that he and I no longer made up stories together. Where had our story stopped?

I shook my head vaguely.

"Was I like that, too?" he asked.

"You?"

"Was I tied down?" He looked straight into my eyes.

Night was plastered against the window where the curtain hadn't been pulled, spying on us with bated breath. Trees in the yard, having shed all their leaves, stood blacker than the darkness; the blood vessels of Night, they pulsated soundlessly.

"Gee, I dunno." Why was this the only answer I could give him? My voice sounded like the halfhearted mumble of someone distracted.

A flock of birds whirred into flight, and Night shivered. Bird-pecked fruit with rotting wounds lay scattered atop the leaves blanketing the yard. The leaves shifted, trampled by unseen feet. Somewhere, an abandoned bird left behind was frantically beating a broken wing. Even knowing that its wing would only be further lacerated, the injury made worse, the bird could not stop clinging to the knife-edged air.

Holding the coffee cup, which was my wife's, in her left hand, the woman resumed speaking into her phone.

"Okay? So you be sure to set her straight. If Mother says crazy stuff, you've got to set her straight. No, I'm not going anywhere! Is she still saying that? I'm just taking a little breather. I'll be back in a week. Tell her that, okay? I've never once tried to run away. Never, since before I was even born. I just endured patiently. That's right, in that pitch-black, cramped place! How can she say such a thing? I mean, how can she say that when *she* was trying to get rid of *me*?"

The woman was now shrieking and swinging her arm as if to drive away someone in front of her by throwing coffee on them. Her breasts heaved. Coffee flew in the air. She slurped from the cup and went on.

"But don't tell her that. Please don't." Pause. "That's right, it's unnecessary. You might only confuse her more. All you need to do is set her straight the minute she says something crazy." Pause. "That's it. Yes, make sure you set *that* straight. The idea that I tried to escape from her womb is ridiculous. After all, I was in there. I ought to know!"

The vibrations of the high-speed train had a numbing effect. Above that steady hum, the woman's rough, agitated breathing came and went. Around her lips was a thin layer of downy hair the color of withered grass.

"Why would my mother lie like that?"

Sensing a change in the woman's voice, my wife turned to look at her. The woman's eyes were focused on my wife's belly. How long had she been staring? Her gaze wrapped around my wife, her voice stuck to her.

"*She* was trying to escape, not me. She wanted to leave me behind and take off somewhere. It was her! But I didn't let her get away. No ma'am. I hung on tight to the umbilical cord and wouldn't let go. I gritted my teeth and hung on. No way was I letting go until I got born."

She threw her head back and laughed uproariously. Shaking, she spat out fragments of words and laughter: "*Ha-ha*...yeah, right...no, no teeth yet...*ha-ha-ha.*"

Her eyeballs seemed ready to pop. Laughter foamed in her like egg whites in a mixing bowl. Her eyes were still glued to my wife's belly as her mouth sprayed white laughter-foam. "Right, right. It's so bizarre. Imagine—killed before you've been born!"

My wife was giggling, too. The foam of laughter was spreading.

"Killed before you've been born!" repeated the woman, flushing beet-red. Whether the words were directed at the person on the other end of the line, at my wife, or at her belly, my wife wasn't sure.

She stroked her belly, winding the woman's gaze around her fingers.

Laughing shrilly, my son collapsed on the sofa cushion. It was printed with an illustration of the family of Babar the Elephant, a favorite of his. He held the innocent-faced Babar tight in his arms and laughed so hard he shook all over. It sounded almost as if he were trying to dislodge something burrowing deep inside him by spraying it with bullet-like fragments of laughter.

I may have thought I would lend him a hand. I grabbed

an ankle that was waving wildly, like a rabbit caught in a trap, and dangled him in the air. Instead of blood, he kept leaking laughter. Even hanging upside down, he was laughing.

He loved to be held upside down or to ride on someone's shoulders. Every time we went to visit my wife's parents, her younger brother would be there, and my son would beg him for a ride. My brother-in-law is a giant, over six and a half feet tall.

The laughter emanating from my son's upside-down body changed at some point to sobs.

I laid him on the sofa, as if tossing him. On his belly, he pressed his face into the cushion and wept. Babar, distorted by the pressure of the boy's face, was at a loss. Dusk stole back into the living room, slipping through the weak light from the bulb and gathering comfortingly around my son's trembling shoulders. Even Night seemed critical of me.

A dog howled in the distance. Another dog howled as if in reply. Others joined. I stared out the window but couldn't see the woods in the darkness. All I saw was myself, in the glass, a menacing look in my eyes. The dogs had formed a pack and were chasing their quarry, cornering it. The taut surface of the night was torn to shreds by their fangs.

My son was sitting on the sofa, hugging the cushion. His cheeks were drenched with tears and his eyes were swollen, as if he'd been crying for hours. *Aren't you making a little too much of this*, I started to say, but thought better of it.

"I shouldn't have done that," I said. "I'm sorry."

"Daddy."

"What?"

He wasn't looking at me anymore. His eyes were bleary, at the mercy of whatever entered his line of vision.

"Dogs don't eat them. Chickens and geese. Know why?"

"Why dogs don't eat chickens and geese?" I repeated.

He nodded.

The farmhouses around the woods all had chickens and geese that ranged free. Every single house also had a dog. And come to think of it, I had never seen a farm dog chained up.

Poultry sauntered in flocks before the dogs' eyes, rear ends waving as if issuing a challenge: *Eat me. Come on, eat me.* So why didn't the dogs attack? However well trained they might be, surely sometimes they sank their teeth into a bird for the hell of it. Then why keep a dog in the first place? To chase off foxes? No, not only that.

To keep away the greedy imps who come under the cover of Night to steal not only fowl but also little children.

The farmer who rented us the isolated house where we lived would from time to time tell us stories about the imps, along with other centuries-old lore of the woods. One day, he and I were in his yard standing under a walnut tree. The rich array of branches and green leaves overhead formed a canopy, concealing the sky with an intricate arabesque design.

"C'mon, it can't be true, can it?" I said, turning toward him.

The farmer nodded. As usual, the wrinkles around his mouth left me uncertain whether he was smiling or not. A breeze stirred, swaying leaf shadows on his face. The soft leaf-shadow curtain wrapping around him—and of course around me as well—screened us from each other. Behind that torn curtain, he seemed to be laughing.

Outsiders that we were, the farmer and his wife found many ways to show us kindness. That day, he had called and invited me over to take my pick of a bumper crop of eggplant and zucchini. His farm was just under an hour's drive from our house at the edge of the woods. I had parked the car, taken out the stroller, and pushed it over the rough ground toward the entrance to the house, my infant son squealing in excitement at every jolt.

As I listened to the farmer, my son, who had been in such a jolly mood, suddenly began bawling loud enough to rip the air into shreds.

The farmer slapped his forehead. "O-ho!"

I rocked the stroller. "Your mother just fed you. What's wrong?"

My son leaned his head back to get away from the thin, dancing shadows and went on crying.

The farmer bent down to peer into the stroller and then looked up at me. "Sorry, I shouldn't have brought it up around him."

But my son hadn't been set off by tales of imps coming and going in the night. He was too small to understand.

We often stopped by the farmer's place on our strolls. Once he learned to walk, our son toddled gleefully after the chickens in the yard.

"Goodness. He thinks he's another hen!" My wife laughed.

An idea popped into my head. "We'll have to get a dog."

She gave me a blank look.

"To fend off imps," I said with a knowing wink.

"But we don't have any chickens or geese." She frowned.

"Children get stolen, too, you know."

"Goodness." Her eyes twinkled with mischief. "Better not let down your guard just because you're grown up, either."

"That settles it, we need a dog. We're all in danger."

"Yeah, right." She laughed uproariously, though I wasn't sure what was so funny.

But we didn't get a dog. Even though we had plenty of opportunities.

The farmer had two bitches of mixed breed–Mardi and Éclair. Several years before, Mardi had had a litter of four. Three pups soon found homes, leaving behind only a female they named Avril.

Our son never asked for a puppy, not when he found out Mardi was pregnant, nor when he saw the little ones at her side. He loved Avril as if she were his own, but he never gave us trouble by carrying on and begging to take her home.

My grandmother had a dog named Mémé, a shaggy mixed-breed bitch with a brown and white coat who was half-paralyzed in old age.

"She can't go on the walks she loves so much, poor thing." Grandma would put Mémé in a wheelchair she'd acquired and push her around outdoors. In the winter, she would wind a scarf around Mémé's head and neck and wrap her snugly in a blanket. When passers-by saw that the person seated in the wheelchair had a long furry snout and dangling tongue, they reacted with shock or amusement, turning back again and again for another look. Sometimes you'd hear a nervous giggle.

Grandma paid no attention. With the serious air of one attending the creation of the world, she'd push the wheelchair straight toward a destination she could clearly visualize. And as often as not she got lost.

Even if Mémé had remembered the way, she had no means of steering Grandma in the right direction. Unable to walk on her own, all Mémé could do was let herself be taken wherever Grandma went. But as long as she was with Grandma, Mémé probably didn't mind.

After Grandma died, Mémé drooled and trembled, snorting as she called out for her. Her cloudy white eyes couldn't have seen Grandma any longer, and her stuffed-up nose couldn't have picked up Grandma's scent. Her mournful howl was heartrending. She struggled to get up and go in search of Grandma, but her hindquarters, as immovable as a tree stump, prevented her from so much as crawling. Eventually, borne away on waves of ever-longer sleep, she went to be with Grandma.

Once, around the time Mémé's weakening hind legs began to cross if she tried to walk, I saw Grandma administering a small pill to the dog. I asked what kind of pill it was.

"It's *the* pill," said Grandma, breaking the beige pill in half with a fingernail. She held Mémé's snout–over the dog's objections–with one hand and pushed the half of a pill into her mouth with her fingers.

"The pill?"

"Well, we can't have her getting pregnant, can we?" She held out her palm for Mémé to lick.

"Huh. So there's a contraceptive pill for dogs?"

"Of course there is." Without looking at me, Grandma added offhandedly, "This one's for people, though."

"The pill that people use works on dogs?"

"Of course it does." Grandma kept her eyes on Mémé. Her answer had finality.

"But Mémé doesn't need it anymore, does she?"

Grandma seemed not to hear this. Mémé's bent ears twitched.

"And where did you get contraceptive pills for people anyway, Grandma?" I pressed.

She was silent, scratching under Mémé's chin. Mémé's eyes were half-closed in bliss. Grandma's eyes softened in satisfaction.

"If they have pills for dogs, why not use those?" I persisted. "There's no reason to give her people pills." I may have intended what I said next as a joke, to tease her. "*You* certainly don't need them, do you, Grandma?"

Again, no reply.

"Grandma." Back then I didn't know when to stop.

"You don't take them, you get pregnant. That's that."

Mémé's ears stiffened. She looked up into Grandma's face.

Were Grandma's words directed at me, or at Mémé, lying motionless on her belly in front of Grandma...or at herself?

My son was on the sofa with his head pressed into the cushion in his arms. He looked up. His tears had dried. He asked the same question as before.

"You know why they don't eat them? Dogs? Eat chickens and geese?"

"Hmm, I don't know."

"I know," he said. He was speaking as if squashing tiny insects with his thumb. "I know."

"Why is it? Tell Daddy." I think I was less interested in the topic than in the fact that, for the first time in a while, he wanted to talk to me.

"I saw it. When I went to play at Uncle's place, all of a

sudden the chickens started squawking. Really loud. The air was full of white feathers."

He beat the cushion on his lap—was that his imitation of chickens beating their wings?—while saying "*Ga ga ga ga ga ga*" in an odd-sounding voice. Dust flew vigorously into the air, but was swiftly swallowed by dusk, lurking with its mouth wide open.

"Why were the chickens making so much noise?" I asked.

"It was Avril. Avril was chasing them. I saw her. Yeah, she was running around the chickens like crazy. She liked raising a ruckus."

"Avril was making mischief." I frowned.

"Then she did something bad," he said sadly. "She ran up and bit one of the chickens on the neck, sank her teeth in." He hugged the cushion with all his might.

"Oh no!" I put a hand to my forehead. "What happened to the chicken?"

"It didn't move. The head was hanging from Avril's mouth." He laid his chin on the cushion. "And then all of a sudden Uncle was there. He said 'bad dog' over and over. I was really scared. He was like a different person. Avril knew he was mad at her. She didn't move. Even when Uncle went to the barn, she just stood there with her head down. But she never let go of the chicken."

"Why did Uncle go to the barn?"

"He went to get a bag. A big old leather bag. And he was carrying a hard wooden stick. Then he said to me,

'Hadn't you better go home?' I told him I was okay, but he kept on asking. I said no, even though, really, I wanted to go home. But I couldn't move. Just like Avril. Because Uncle didn't seem like Uncle anymore. Somebody else had gotten inside the regular Uncle. His face looked like he had a stomachache. I was scared. Avril was shaking, too. Shaking hard. Drooling. The chicken in her mouth was shaking, too. 'Hurry up and let it go!' I shouted. All the other chickens were making a terrible racket. Geese, too."

Remaining on the sofa, he bent his head back and flapped his outspread arms. His small calves beat against the leather. Was he imitating the excited poultry? But it looked to me as if he were in water, about to go under. He was sticking his head up between the relentlessly pounding waves, desperately seeking air. He flailed blindly to keep from sinking to the bottom, gasping for breath. Over and over he wiped his eyes with the palm of his hand.

"I asked Uncle what he was going to do. To Avril. He didn't answer. He went over to her. Avril didn't move. She couldn't stand up anymore. She was lying kind of flat, her head down. But she was still holding the chicken in her mouth. Shaking so hard, probably her mouth wouldn't open. *Uncle, don't do it!*"

On the sofa, my son stuck out his small arms and pulled back his head, hiding from disaster.

It's okay. I started toward him to comfort him. *Don't be afraid, Daddy's here.* But in the eyes he turned toward me, terror was spreading in dark, widening waves.

"Stop it...stop it..."

His voice sounded like fingernails scraping the surface of the air. He would not let me get close to him.

Daddy's here, I wanted to say again. *There's nothing to be scared of.* But I couldn't speak.

Frantically, my son waved his hands in front of him. Then he put his palms to his face and shook his head fiercely.

No, it's me, Daddy, I wanted to tell him, but he kept shaking his head.

He raised his head slowly, cautiously. What he saw, I don't know. Whatever it was, it was something other than me. I could not bear to see that look.

His voice sounded far away.

"But it was too late. Uncle was already holding Avril by the neck. Avril looked really small now, and Uncle's hand looked really big. He ripped the hen from Avril's mouth and put it in the bag. Then he put Avril in the bag, too, and tied it tight. It happened really fast."

He stood up on the sofa. He gripped a corner of the cushion and held it out toward me.

"Inside the bag Avril started to struggle. I thought maybe the chicken had come back to life and was fighting with her." He shook the cushion in his hand. "But that wasn't it. Avril was squirming and struggling to get out of the bag. Uncle picked up the stick from the ground. Then the other chickens beat their wings and carried on, and everything got even noisier than before. Lots of dust went up in the air. I couldn't open my eyes. *Ga ga ga ga ga*—they made an awful racket. I had to cover my ears with my hands."

He covered his ears with his hands and crouched on the sofa, hunched over.

I laid a hand gently on my son's shoulder. He let me do that. Tremors shook the surface of his body in ripples. He mumbled something, but because he was shivering, the sounds disintegrated on his tongue before they could coalesce into words. The sounds were broken, unintelligible; they were the sound of something breaking.

He brushed my hand away and cried out: "*Wham! Wham! Wham!* I heard a terrible sound—*wham!* It surprised me, so I opened my eyes and saw Uncle raising the stick."

Like an uncoiling spring, he jumped to his feet on the sofa and waved an arm. His eyes were wide. But they held no terror. They held nothing. He seemed to see nothing. Or rather, his eyes rejected everything. To erase all he didn't want to see, instead of shutting his eyes he wiped out its existence.

"Uncle beat the bag with the stick. Avril was screaming. But Uncle didn't stop. He hit the bag again and again. His face was scary. He was somebody else. I closed my eyes right away but I could still see. He didn't stop. Every time Avril got hit with the stick, there was a terrible sound, and she screamed. The bag was on the ground, moving, all squishy. The hens were squawking like they'd lost their minds. I was scared. I covered my ears, but I could still hear them. It felt like they were going crazy inside my head. I was really scared that Avril might die, getting hit like that. I felt like I might go all squishy, too. But Uncle didn't stop. He didn't stop hitting the bag with the stick."

He threw the cushion on the floor and jumped down on it from the sofa. He lost his balance and pitched forward. He tried to get up, but hugged himself as if he'd been struck hard by something, maybe a stick, and squatted down. He lifted his face and blinked over and over.

I reached out to help him up, but without a glance at my hand he stood up weakly and started to walk, dragging one leg. His shoulders heaved, and he seemed about to collapse. For a moment he wandered around the living room, and when he came back by the sofa he came to a halt and stomped on the cushion as hard as he could, again and again. His mouth was half-open and skewed, but he made no sound that I could hear. No groaning or sobbing or howling or anything.

He grabbed the cushion in both hands, threw it on the sofa, and attacked it with his fists. That went on for some time.

His shoulders were heaving. Even then, the heavy breathing that shook him so hard it seemed he might break was inaudible to me.

He didn't stop. With every pound of his fists, the cushion seemed to writhe.

I was shocked that my son claimed to have seen that incident with his own eyes. When she was still a puppy, poor Avril had dashed out into the road, gotten hit by a car, and had to have her left front leg amputated. She could barely walk, let alone run around. She was always sprawled limply by the steps leading into the farmer's house, dozing. Sometimes, as if she'd just remembered something, she would twist her neck and lick her stomach as if lapping melted butter. It was impossible for me to believe that Avril could have caught a chicken or goose.

As I listened to my son tell the story—captivated—I realized that I had heard it before. And then it came to me: the story was my wife's. It was a scene *she* had witnessed. For some reason, I was satisfied with that explanation.

When she'd told me the story, we had been in the kitchen. In the middle of the table was a huge pile of beans she'd brought home from the farm, and we were de-stringing them. When people are engaged in manual work like that, their expressions become serious. But her eyes contained something heavier and darker.

She noticed me watching her and sighed, laid the bean she was holding on the table, and slowly stroked her belly, which was just starting to show.

"This is bad for the baby," she said.

"Is it?" I stood up, went over to the small radio atop

the microwave, and turned it off. *Jacob's Ladder* had been playing.

"Not that," she said, looking up. "I didn't mean the music."

"What, then?"

She looked down without answering my question. Addressing her belly, she whispered, "I'm sorry I made you see that, it was terrible." She kept stroking her belly, as if to soothe not only her anxious feelings but also the child's.

When the farmer had called, I'd been out in the yard with the hose, watering all the apple trees. My wife had gone over alone to get some vegetables and eggs.

That's when she saw it.

A hen being attacked by the other hens.

Part of the yard became a surging white swell, its boundaries shifting by the second. In the center was the struggling, wounded hen. There was a spot of blood on her back, which had become the target of the hens who were relentlessly pecking at it, as if spurred to attack by the color.

One beak tore at feathers around the wound. The hen cried out pitifully and tried to get away. To no avail, though, as another hen swiftly cut off her path and another beak immediately struck. But the eyes of the attacking hens betrayed no animus. They were empty, blank, intent merely on the task. They did not do their violence all at once but inflicted injury by degrees. One hen, then another, would peck at the victim, while others were distracted and indifferent. As the wounded hen weakened, her fate grew certain. The white swell that was the attack bulged and pulsated misshapenly but never broke. It was the wound, the blood of the wound, that they stabbed at unhesitatingly with their beaks, creating the wound, tearing at it, enlarging it. The existence in their circle of one so weak and pitiful was not to be borne; the weak had to be expunged, wiped out. The bloodied hen staggered, stood still, swaying, then crumpled and lay unmoving. Instantly, the white cluster broke up and the hens fanned out across the yard, leaving on the feather-littered ground the single hen lying in place like a stain.

Avril did not attack the hen. Avril did not have her neck grabbed by the farmer, and she wasn't thrown in the bag. Avril hadn't even been born yet. Neither had our son. He was the one my wife had been expecting. Since his birth, she and I had never spoken of that incident. And yet he knew about it.

Had he somehow witnessed it?

Impossible.

Then was he listening as she told me the story in the kitchen? Listening from inside her, with bated breath?

She'd said something to her belly.

"Huh?" I said. "What'd you say?"

"You must have been scared," she said, with her hand against her belly, addressing it. Then she looked up at me with a sad smile. "See, he's trembling."

"Trembling?"

"Yes. Here, feel."

I crouched down beside her and put one hand on her shoulder, the other gently on her belly. She put her hand over mine.

"I'm so sorry," she whispered to her belly. "You were scared, weren't you?"

I looked at her as she bent her head down.

"You were scared, weren't you?" she repeated and gripped my hand tight.

It was not our unborn child who was trembling. It was my wife. I said nothing. In the end, it was all the same.

"You were scared, weren't you?" I said, stroking her belly.

As the train went through the tunnel, my wife couldn't hear what the woman sitting next to her was saying. The screeching of the coach grew louder. The waves of sound became many-layered walls surrounding her, distancing her from the world. The surfaces of her clothing shook on their own. Could eardrums comprehend the meaning of the sounds that set them vibrating? Was the woman really speaking?

The man across the aisle, the one who had glared when the woman took out her phone and started talking, was fast asleep. His seat would not recline, so to make himself comfortable, he had raised the armrest and stretched out crosswise over two seats. His head was bent back, and one leg poked into the aisle. His mouth was slightly open—just enough that it made you want to slip in a coin.

My wife knew that somewhere in the long tunnel they would enter another country.

She glanced sideways at the woman next to her, who was resting her chin in her hand, her elbow on the sill, apparently gazing out the window. But the window showed only the reflection of her own face, staring back at her, aghast. A face that had at some point acquired deep wrinkles of fatigue. In a matter of hours she had seemingly aged years.

Watching the cup of coffee jostle on the table in front of her, my wife grew uneasy.

"We're there," she heard the woman say.

By now the train must have entered the other country, a land where the language was all but unintelligible to her. It surprised her that she could still understand the woman. But then, a person's language doesn't change just because they've crossed a border. She smiled to herself. "Yes, we're there," she repeated in a low voice, making sure. It was still a foreign language to her, but one not lost to her. She could repeat it.

Her throat was extremely dry, and her body felt hot—as if she herself and not the other woman had been talking on the phone all this time. Her underarms were unpleasantly wet with perspiration.

She reached out and picked up the coffee cup. There was still some coffee in it. She moistened her dry lips. It didn't taste good. She made a face.

Suddenly, all sounds reverberated loudly. She looked up in surprise and was struck by a flood of light streaming in through the window across the aisle. It was a giant band of gold and silver, with variegated sounds blending, yielding to one another, then disappearing. Light filled her body and overflowed to become one with all the other light in the world. The window ledge, the edge of the seat, and the face of the sleeping man, all shone like molten metal, so bright she could scarcely open her eyes.

The train was passing over a trestle above a wide river. In the pale sky were a few wisps of cloud. As the train rumbled across, the river reflected the tranquility of the sky.

From the window on the left she could see a fine road running alongside the river, supported by tall concrete girders. The road, which crossed the trestle at a right angle, was chock full of vehicles, all of them trucks, headed this way like a file of ants. Military vehicles, she thought. Their wheels seemed not to be turning; rather, the road itself was a conveyor belt. The flatbeds of the trucks were full of soldiers. At least, that's what they looked like to her. But what was their destination? She turned to look out the window on the right to see where the road went.

The woman was leaning forward and looking out the window, blocking her view. The windows didn't open, yet the woman's flaming silver hair danced as if caught in a gust of wind. My wife craned her neck and looked out through the part of the window that wasn't blocked.

Suddenly, like the moment after a large balloon pops, sound was swallowed by nothingness. All she could see was trailing smoke. The train had crossed all the way over the river, and the familiar vibrations started up again. She had a nagging feeling, one completely at odds with the peaceful scenery of gently undulating hills, an uneasy feeling that those hills might come crashing down like angry billows.

Crashing down. That was happening in real life to the road.

She saw it. The road didn't lead anywhere. It just stopped. Was it unfinished? She didn't think so. It had been destroyed. Could the trucks not see where they were headed? Why didn't they stop?

The train did not stop. It kept barreling forward. The sounds diminished even as the anxiety within her swelled. In the seat beside her, the woman's rotund body became the embodiment of all things incomprehensible and, devouring the surrounding space, seemed to take on more and more flesh. The woman's arm spilling over the armrest now pressed with slight heat against her belly. She felt suffocated.

She reached out, slipped a hand into the swelling folds of flesh, and found the woman's hand. A dry, cold hand. She squeezed it. The hand lacked resistance, like the body of a small animal in a deep sleep from which it would not awaken. It lay limp and motionless in her hand.

She closed her eyes. After a while, she could no longer tell which way her seat was facing. The distance between her and the swirl of sounds shrank. The sounds reminded her of the murmur of a large river flowing slowly through the depths of the night. The flow of water, hidden during the day, spreading widely, unbounded, in the darkness. Was the murmur of water so much clearer because her senses were sharpened at night?

No, that wasn't it. She shook her head a little. Night itself was acutely sensitive. Sensitive to the trembling of every creature, however small, in the world that it embraced. That's what she thought, her eyelids firmly shut.

I drank some freshly brewed coffee in the kitchen. I knew it would keep me from sleeping, but I was wide awake, as if my son's excitement had transferred to me.

It wasn't as if there was some reason I *had* to sleep. Besides, who knew when the phone might ring?

I'd had a tough time getting my son to go to sleep. The sound of his crying had beat me down until I felt like crying myself.

Why did he cry so hard now? There would be plenty of time for tears later. Or perhaps he had already figured out that the day was coming when he would not have tears enough for the multitude of sorrows and pains that lay ahead, and his fear and anguish over that apprehension was making him cry.

Had I been like this as a child? I couldn't remember.

Anyway, he had exhausted himself and should have been sleepy, but something rampaging inside him resisted sleep.

Was it because while he slept, a troop of imps might come under cover of darkness and carry him off?

My wife and I diverted ourselves by talking about the legends of the woods, without coming to any conclusion. But I couldn't recall ever having told our son about the imps.

Of course, it was perfectly possible that he had pressed a brand-new ear against the soft wall of the womb, so sensitive to vibration, and listened in private to the words my wife's body remembered.

But there were things he couldn't know. Things I had never told my wife.

Once I went to the farmer's place to borrow a scythe to cut the grasses in our yard. Yes, a scythe, like the one in the hands of the Grim Reaper.

It was a summer day so bright and hot that it seemed the Grim Reaper himself would have succumbed. When I got out of the car, I felt dizzy, as if I'd been clobbered with a nightstick. Then I reasoned: if Eros, the giver of love, never feels love himself, then perhaps the Grim Reaper, who brings death, will never know death. I considered these notions vaguely. Though the road was completely dry, the sunshine was so dense that dust had no room to rise. From there to the farmer's house wasn't far, but my feet dragged, as if I were wading in water.

As always, Mardi and Éclair came bounding out to greet me. Their tongues hung out, and slobber dripped from their mouths. The farmer was sitting in a wooden chair under the eaves, waiting for me. Avril was missing from her usual spot on the front steps. The sun was probably too intense even for her. I saw her raise her head in the dimness just inside the house.

"Hot, isn't it?" the farmer said, getting up from his chair. "This heat is too much."

"Right." I nodded, wiping my forehead. I had intended to borrow the scythe and get right back home. But the farmer felt like talking.

"Come have a drink," he said, stepping indoors.

I followed him inside.

The kitchen was dim. A big fly was darting around the room. The windows facing the yard were open, yet the fly did not know how to get out. The farmer brought out two wineglasses and filled them half full of red wine. He filled a porcelain pitcher with tap water, which he then added to the wine. I drank the diluted wine in one gulp. When I set my glass back on the table, without a word he refilled it. I picked it up, leaned back against the white kitchen wall, and waited.

He scarcely touched his own wineglass.

With his hands stuck in the front pockets of his jeans, he perched on the windowsill and began to talk. His eyes didn't meet mine. He talked as if he were speaking to someone standing behind me.

"Did you ever meet my mother?" he asked.

I shook my head. His mother had died before my wife and I moved here.

"I had two brothers," he said. "One older, one younger."

I nodded. This was news to me.

"Out in the barn," he began, turning around and pointing somewhere I could not see, "we had a pair of bulls. Back when I was little."

The fly was crawling around on the bell of the wine-glass on the table without the slightest regard for the effect of gravity on its tiny body.

"Before that, we had horses," he continued, turning back to me. "The war made us poor. Same thing happened to all the farming families around here. My dad lost an arm, and my mother lost two children–my brothers. It's as if they got swindled. 'We were better off in the last century,' Mother used to say. She was bitter. We got poorer and poorer, and in the end they had to sell the last horse. That was a tragedy for the family."

He now picked up his wineglass, took a sip, and stepped toward the table, diagonally across from me.

"What kind of horse was it?" I asked, looking up at him. His features stood out clearly, as if chiseled, in the sun coming through the window.

"I don't know." He set the glass back down on the table with a small, dry clatter. "It was before I was born.

Mother talked about it till her dying day. What a blow it was for the family to have to sell that horse. She went on about it, over and over, like she did when she recited a spell to stop lightning."

He came a few steps closer to me and stopped.

"Lightning?" I said.

"Yes. You know how lightning can strike in a storm? If it comes down the chimney, it can get inside the house and wreak havoc, like a snake. The ashes in the fireplace fly out, the curtains erupt in flames. Chairs and tables get overturned. Sometimes windowpanes break. The house is a mess afterward; it looks like a drunk went on a rampage."

"Do such things really happen?" His stories always amazed me.

"Yes, in the old days. In the old days, used to happen all the time." His eyelids were half-closed, as if staring at some faraway place inside him. Then he looked up and shrugged. "Of course, I never saw it myself. But that's what I heard."

I looked at his face and nodded. The bags under his eyes were wet with perspiration and slightly red.

"It's as good as a memory." He made a slicing gesture with his hand. "Appears suddenly, cuts through the darkness. Right? But even if you can drive away lightning, you can't drive away a memory. Know what I mean?"

I nodded.

"Mother never got over the loss of her sons." He was stroking his cheek as if searching for whiskers he'd missed shaving. "It was a, what do you call it...a *trauma*, that's it. A family trauma. No one spoke of it."

He was standing just to my left. It was always like that. We would start out facing each other, and in the course of the conversation he would move, little by little, so that we ended up side by side, our shoulders touching. I couldn't see his face; I could only hear his voice. I couldn't see where his voice was coming from. I couldn't see where the silence was coming from. I couldn't see, but I listened. His shoulder nudged mine several times as if seeking support, testing it. Our contact was firm and gentle. I found it warm and human.

He began speaking again. "My big brother was quite a bit older than me. He was no soldier. He joined the Resistance. All the young men around here did. He went into the woods with his comrades and was never heard from again. Never came home."

"How old was he?" I asked.

"I'm not sure. Not twenty. Seventeen or eighteen, maybe."

"How old were you?"

"We were ten years apart, so I'd have been around eight."

"Then you remember him well."

"Oh yes. But I never understood why he disappeared. I pestered my mother, wanting to know where he'd gone. The deaths hadn't been confirmed. Everybody wanted to believe that someday they'd all come home. Maybe that's why Mother said those things, that it was because of imps in the woods. They took him, she said."

"Imps?"

"Yes. You know about the castle in the woods, don't you?"

"I do, but we haven't been there yet."

The farmer chuckled. "We call it a castle, but it's not much of one. It's deep in the woods, hard to find. Used to be the mansion of the landowning family that controlled this area. During the war, it was the headquarters of the Resistance. So Mother wasn't entirely wrong in saying that my brother was taken away by imps."

"How so?"

"When I was little, they told us the castle was a den of imps. 'Cruel, cunning imps live there, so don't go near,' they said. 'Go too far into the woods and the imps'll get you,' was the warning."

I turned and looked at the farmer.

He nudged me a bit with his shoulder, then went on, "My younger brother was stillborn. The umbilical cord was wound around his neck. Not that I saw it with my own eyes. That's what I heard. So, no baby. Mother's belly went back to what it had been before. Sagging like the belly of the cow we got instead of a horse. But there was no baby. *Where's the baby?* I wanted to ask her. *Where'd my big brother go, huh? Where'd my baby brother go, huh? Where are they? Huh?*"

With every "*huh?*" his shoulder pressed hard against

mine. Then his shoulder grew still.

"But I couldn't ask. I said nothing. Because of what I saw."

"What did you see?" I asked, shooing off the fly with one hand; it kept landing on my face, as if to confirm its contours.

He replied with a question. "Is it true that if a baby doesn't take the breast, the mother's milk stops?"

I looked at him. He looked back at me, one eyebrow raised. I gave him the first answer that came to mind. "Yes, isn't it?"

"Then it's true? My little ones were born such a long time ago, I can't remember how it was. It's not the sort of thing you can easily ask, either."

"Didn't you just become a grandfather?" I asked. The farmer's son, an elementary school teacher, lived with his girlfriend in a town about an hour's drive away. I had recently heard that she'd had a baby.

The farmer laughed and gave my shoulder a slight push. "What, I should ask my son's girlfriend to show me her breasts?"

"Maybe not," I said, smiling.

"Your second child is due soon, isn't it?" he asked.

"Not for a while yet. But your story, tell me, what was it you saw?"

"Yes, I saw it all right. Woke up in the night. Needed to take a leak. Back then toilets were outdoors, you see. When I went past my mother's room, light was coming from under her door. I cautiously pushed the door open and peeked in. She was up, sitting on the bed. That's when I saw it. Her shadow took up the whole wall, swaying like it was being blown by a gust of wind. You know how kids put a sheet over their head to look like a ghost? The shadow looked like that. Only it wasn't white, it was pitch black. Inside it, there were shapes moving around. Shoving each other like they were playing. Slowly they embraced my mother from behind, whispering. She was sitting still, listening to whatever the whispers were saying, in voices that made me think of someone licking the little hairs on the back of your neck. Gave me goosebumps. What were they telling her? I couldn't imagine. And her body was so white. I mean, she had nothing on. And I saw it spilling out, right out of her breasts. Milk, I mean, out of her nipples. It didn't stop coming. I thought for a second she was injured, maybe bleeding or something. But it wasn't blood. No, it was milk. In the dim light of the room, the drops of milk shone silver, and her eyes, too. Her eyes were wet. She kept wiping away the milk from her breasts with a cloth, but every time she brought the cloth up to her eyes, her breasts would spill more and more milk. Then the big shadow embracing her rocked like waves, as if it were happy. I was terrified. I still needed to pee, but I was too scared to go outside. Because suddenly I thought of the imps."

The farmer shivered and stretched. For a second, our shoulders parted company. Then he returned his shoulder to mine and continued the story.

"Until then I'd never given the imps much thought. But I did sort of believe they'd carted my baby brother off to the woods. Of course, my mother never said any such thing. She never said what happened to him, and she never said he was taken by imps. I never asked her where he'd gone, either. But I knew it then, beyond a doubt."

Yet from the way he spoke, whatever he knew, he hadn't known it "then," as a child, but only "now," sharing it with me.

"Yes, even when my big brother disappeared, Mother may never have said anything about imps taking him off to the woods. I may only have imagined it. But I have a distinct memory. I remember hearing he'd been taken. Maybe it wasn't my mother who said it, maybe it was somebody else. Both brothers disappeared. Who was first to go, I don't remember. But I got the picture. It was all clear to me. Yes, yes."

The farmer's shoulder pressed mine persistently, seeking a sign that I was listening.

"See, I knew. I knew it wasn't my big brother the imps had taken away, but my baby brother. My big brother had gone looking for him. I idolized my big brother. He was good to me. So I was jealous. I thought, *He went off looking for our little brother without ever having laid eyes on him?* I was so jealous, I planned how I'd get back at him after he brought the baby home. Crazy, huh? I thought if it wasn't for the baby, he'd never have disappeared. But Mother didn't tell me anything. Never said a word. She always had a dark, brooding look on her face. Which was only natural. She, more than anyone, wanted to know where her firstborn son had gone. And I couldn't ask my dad. He lost an arm in the war, and after he came back he became a drunk. He'd get drunk and try to hit my mother, swinging his arm, only to find it was gone. He'd open his eyes wide and stare into space, thunderstruck." The farmer gave a snort of laughter. His shoulder shook with laughter, causing mine to shake, and I laughed, too.

"Of course, it wasn't any imp that took my big brother away," said the farmer, after he stopped laughing. "My brother and his comrades were betrayed and executed. Tied with their hands behind their backs, lined up along the road through the woods, and hanged from trees. I didn't see it. That's what I heard. Who betrayed them? Farmers from a nearby village. People I'd seen around. People who went to the same school. Why they did it, I don't know. For a while after that, I was afraid of the dark. I'd think, *There are imps out there, watching us from the depths of night, and if they come for me what'll I do? But if I can see my big brother, let 'em come*, I'd think, getting excited. Then it would be even harder to sleep."

We stood and looked out the window, still shoulder to shoulder. The forms of all things stood out clearly. Dust that hovered over chicken feathers and squawks in defiance of the flow of time; a bicycle with a rusty chain, leaning against a wooden fence with peeling white paint;

trees whose names I didn't know, planted along the road in front of the house; green fields beneath birds like a scattering of black sparks high in the sky: each thing was present with a sense of reality so intense that we could have taken them in our hands and crushed them. The fly buzzing around the room, pushed away by the stream of light pouring through the window, clung persistently to the farmer's and then my sweaty skin as if asking again and again how to get out the window.

That afternoon, I tried to mow the grass with the scythe I'd borrowed from the farmer.

The grass was knee-high and dense; walking through it was nearly impossible. Nor did I dare step under the trees, where nettles were waiting for an unwary foot.

I swung the scythe with all my might to cut through the thick, green vegetation. I didn't wear a hat, exposing myself to the ferocious sunlight.

Why I embarked on such an effort, I don't really know. Was I hunting for the imps that lay in wait under the blades of grass, spying on us, seeking entry into our lives? I don't think so.

And not that it mattered. Because either I did not have the knack or the scythe was dull. Time and again the blade got caught in the grass. I cursed. My body shook. As did the grass at my feet, shaking with scorn, laughing. Angry and frustrated, I tried to yank the scythe out, but the tall grass wrapped around it like wet hair and wouldn't let go. I fell on my ass. The sky cracked open and laughter rained down.

Sweat dripped from my forehead as pollen swirled up like ash and tiny insects swarmed around me. Worse perhaps was the intense, blinding sunlight. I freed the scythe and swung it in a frenzy. If anyone had been nearby, they'd have been in mortal danger. (Fortunately, my wife and son had gone shopping.) My T-shirt was plastered to my torso, and my jeans stuck to me like a soaked rag. It was unpleasant. That wasn't all. With the pungent smell of cut grass, the hot air became a macabre porridge of offal. It was disgusting, yet it was forced down my throat. And, miserable, I swallowed it.

Trying to drive away the countless hands forcing that thick substance down my throat, I swung the scythe blindly. I couldn't see any hands, because my eyes were shut. The porridge kept coming; I couldn't breathe; I felt nauseated. Tears filled my eyes. Tears or sweat, I couldn't tell which. I felt faint. I swung the scythe as a final form of resistance. My ears rang with the sound of my own gasps. The porridge came back up my throat, filling my mouth with sourness, burning my nose. I dropped the scythe and fell into a violent coughing fit. Every cough took away air; my head grew numb at the core. Through the mist came the sound of mocking laughter. They were trying to stifle their laughter, but I heard it clearly: imps somewhere far off were laughing at my predicament. The sun continued, unimpeded, to pour down light without the least hesitance. No matter how cunning the imps were, where could they possibly find a place to hide in this world so burning with light that I couldn't open my eyes? Ah, but all they needed was the darkness behind my shut eyelids. There they could find all they wanted of endless night.

That night I went to bed with a fever. When I tried to hand the thermometer to my wife, my son snatched it away. He didn't know how to read a thermometer, but he waved away my wife's reaching hand and wouldn't surrender it. I was shut inside thick walls of stone. High atop the walls, their voices mingled in the heavy, enveloping heat. Their voices were far, indistinct.

"I want it!" my son screeched.

Irritated, I barked, "Give it to your mother."

"No, I want it, I want it!"

"Stop that," my wife said firmly. "Give it to me."

I retreated to my despair.

She finally wrested the thermometer away from the boy. "Oh, no! It's 104."

I hadn't had such a high temperature in a long time. My body felt as if it were floating on a bed of hot molten lead. If my arms and legs had come off and drifted away, leaving me behind, I wouldn't have noticed.

The passengers all stood as if they had heard their names called. Like butterflies emerging from chrysalises, one by one they straightened their backs and stood up. No one knew where the voice calling them might be coming from, but in each heart the assurance grew that sooner or later it would be their turn.

The standing passengers put their arms through the sleeves of their coats and jackets, rewound their scarves around their necks, and took down their suitcases, backpacks, and packages from the overhead luggage rack. Languor mingled with restlessness. Shoulders, arms, and sighs brushed against each other. But no eyes met; all eyes were turned in the same direction. What waited there, she did not know.

She raised her head and looked at the faces of the people lined up in the aisle. She tried unsuccessfully to remember if her name had been called or not.

The woman next to her didn't stand. The woman's hand in hers had gone completely cold. Her body appeared to have shrunk a size or two for some reason. Though lacking vitality, she stayed in constant restless motion. Something inside her—something the eye could not see—was moving, seeking a way to escape. Or was the woman herself trying to escape, to free herself from that unseen presence? Under her chocolate-colored sweater, her enormous but now exhausted, drooping breasts were rocking. My wife was tempted to yank the woman's limp hand with all her strength in order to pull out whatever was trapped within her flesh, or to save her from it.

Had the woman's name been called?

Impossible. She shook her head slightly. The woman's name hadn't been called, and neither had hers. Nor would they be. In fact, no one's name had been called.

The passengers in the aisle began to trudge forward, their progress impeded by people on the sides squeezing in at any opportunity. At some point the aisle reached a critical mass and all movement stopped. Still the doors didn't open.

The train began to slow down, approaching its destination. This would be the first, and only, stop.

No need to hurry, she thought. One way or another, they all had to get off. Then, right away, there would be the lines for immigration.

She let go of the woman's hand.

"We're there," she heard a voice say.

"Yes, we're there," she repeated under her breath, as the other passengers began to move forward and disembark.

Now hardly anyone was left in the coach. She stood up, took down her coat from the luggage rack, and slipped her arms through the sleeves. Then she slung the backpack over her shoulders. Glanced at the woman. Stood on tiptoe to check the luggage rack; it was empty. Glanced again at the woman, who was now asleep with her head against the window.

Had whatever had been fighting to get out of the woman's body succeeded? Or had the woman finally been able to escape whatever had refused to let her go?

But between the woman and her lay an impassably huge, deep chasm.

Should she say goodbye? If she called out to the woman now, she feared falling into the chasm, words and all.

She turned and walked away. When she stepped down onto the platform, she followed the people that all moved in one direction.

"We're there." No one was around to hear, but she said the words again in a clear voice. She could see her breath, and it struck her in the face, surprising her a little.

She stopped walking. Then she thrust a hand into her backpack and rummaged for her phone to let them know she'd arrived.

I sat with my elbows propped on the kitchen table, my chin on my fists, and looked out through the open kitchen window. A cloth of deep purple covered the world. Hiding stars in its folds like a thief, borne aloft by the sighs of pursuing Night, the cloth was just about to disappear into the distance.

I wasn't the only one left behind, it seemed. With every repetition of morning, Night was always left behind, stripped naked.

All around me was radiant with the chirping of birds, as they strummed the rays of light coming through the window. The aroma of coffee filled the room.

"Daddy," said my son, finishing his hot milk. He had a white mustache.

"What?"

"See that? Let's call Mommy, okay?"

I noted with some surprise his childish tenor. When telling me about Avril's ordeal, he'd been a small leather bag stuffed with words. Words had come pouring out of him in an uninterrupted stream. Perhaps for that reason, the bag was now empty of all but the first infantile words and cadences that had been put into it.

"See what?"

"That." He pointed. On the shelf over the microwave was the cellphone my wife had forgotten to take with her, right where she had left it.

I laughed, wiping his white mustache with my finger. "Wouldn't work."

Roughly he pushed my finger away, as if it were a pestering bee. "Why not?"

"Why not?" I repeated.

"It's Mommy's, isn't it?"

"Well, yes, it is, but still."

"So let's call Mommy." His eyes glowed with anticipation. "Let's call her!"

"It doesn't work that way. The phone is Mommy's, so unless she has it with her, it's useless. Mommy uses it to call people, or to receive calls from people. *She's* the one who uses it. Understand?"

"Why?" He frowned.

"Even though that phone belongs to Mommy, and it's right here, she, the owner, isn't here. So there's nothing we can do."

"We can't?"

"That's right."

"We can't?"

"It's impossible."

"Then maybe Mommy will call us?" He looked at me, stupefied.

I stared at him, confused by his lack of comprehension; it was as if he had somehow regressed.

"She will. 'Cause it's hers."

I sighed. "You don't get it, do you? Didn't I tell you? Even if Mommy's phone is here, *she's* not here, so unless she calls one of our phones–not this one, but the one in the living room, or Daddy's phone, okay?–unless she does that, we can't talk to her. We have no way to call her with her phone. Okay?"

His head fell, as if an unseen hand were pushing it down. He looked up at me resentfully. Tears were forming in the corners of his eyes.

"I can too call Mommy," he said, sniffling.

"No, you can't." The forcefulness of my tone surprised me.

"Can too." Rubbing his eyes hard with his sleeve, he left the kitchen.

I stood up and refilled my mug with coffee. In the recesses of my numbed head, a phone was ringing.

I turned around and stared disbelievingly at the cellphone quivering on the shelf. The vibrations knocked over a package of cookies propped against the phone, sending them to the floor. As I stooped to retrieve them, I heard energetic footsteps coming from behind me. He came bounding into the kitchen like a dog chasing a ball.

"Mommy! Mommy!" he shouted triumphantly. He grabbed the phone from my hand. "Mommy? Mommy?"

I scarcely existed.

I left him there and went into the living room. I picked up the receiver, which dangled like a criminal just executed by hanging, and pressed it to my ear. I heard his tearful voice: "Mommy? Mommy?"

Silently I hung up the phone.

I went back to where my son was. He looked up at me, dazed, the cellphone pressed tightly against his soft, wet cheek. I crouched down in front of him. He hadn't asked me anything, but I kept my lips pursed as if stuck on an answer, or as if determined not to give one, and stroked the back of his head.

The movement of feet grew sluggish in the disarray of the crowd. Between the many heads blocking her vision, my wife could see a row of booths where customs officials sat. Not all of the booths were occupied, despite the many new arrivals. The large room was filled already with a dull murmur that sounded far away, as from the depths of a dream crushed under the weight of sleep. The murmur in her chest was stolen and, along with the murmurs stolen in the same way from the chests of others, seemed to find resonance high above. An unspoken anxiety moistened the empty cavity like rivulets on a cave wall.

The mass of people approaching the booths was dividing into lines, like a herd of animals being sorted. There was nothing to do but succumb like an animal, stifling a cry that would never be heard, and follow the flow of countless human bodies.

She looked up at the panels hanging from the ceiling, the steel-frame grid, the large silver pipes. The length of the lines seemed to be determined by the passports people held. Her line flowed as smoothly as sand in an hourglass. Nowhere was there a hand to tip the hourglass over.

The adjacent line seemed not to be moving at all. As my wife progressed, the tangle of sobs and sighs that filled the room wound around her.

She could no longer bear it and stopped in place, causing the person behind to bump into her. She turned and apologized. What sort of person that was, whether it was a man or a woman, she could not remember. Had that person clucked impatiently, had they said something polite in response? All she could remember was the tinge of resignation in the person's eyes.

She got out of the line.

Then she heard it more clearly: the faint crying of a baby.

In the other line, her eyes landed on a thin, old woman holding to her breast a baby that was crying so weakly, the sound seemed as if it would trail off at any moment. The old woman was speaking to the baby in words my wife could not understand and shifting her weight from one foot to the other, almost dancing as she tried to distract the baby from its misery.

The baby kept crying, insistent, it seemed, on fighting silence, as if it needed to.

My wife went over to the old woman. The face of the tiny thing wrapped in swaddling clothes was deathly pale. The cheeks were sunken, and beneath the closed eyes there were hollows.

"It's hungry, isn't it," my wife said.

Although the old woman couldn't have understood what my wife said, she nodded.

My wife wiped the baby's cheek, moist from its feeble crying. With wet fingertips, she grasped a tiny, weakly clenched fist. She felt a response to her touch.

"You're hungry, aren't you," she said.

The baby, too, couldn't possibly have understood this, yet its crying gained strength. Or perhaps my wife only imagined it.

No, no, it wasn't her imagination. Slowly, steadily, the crying was growing louder.

My wife proceeded to remove her backpack and place it on the floor. She slipped her right arm out of the sleeve of her coat, and with her left she pulled her sweater and T-shirt up to her neck. Then, unhesitating, she yanked her bra down, and her white breast spilled out. In the cold air, her dark nipple grew taut.

Wordlessly, the old woman handed the infant to her

and watched as she put it to her breast. What the look in the old woman's eyes might mean, my wife neither knew nor cared.

"You're all right now," she cooed.

Yes, now the baby was all right. Upon contact with her soft, warm flesh, it opened its eyes, its mouth. As it greedily sought the warmth of her smooth-skinned breast, its face grew rosy and its eyes shone.

Whether the crying stopped or not, she could not remember. She heard nothing. All she remembered was holding the breast down as it leaped in response to the baby's heartbeat.

The cold sleep that had been about to fall over the baby was in that moment whisked away by the lusty crying that came pouring from the depths of its being. And then, within that tiny body there opened up a large space in which something might be born and never die. For night to become morning, the sky must fill with light, however delicate, and a baby's emptiness must fill with a stream of warmth flowing like sunlight without end.

"You're okay now."

Her pale breast, giving warmth to the baby, received back the baby's warmth and also flushed a rosy red. Breast and baby alike grew warm and plump, becoming one.

THE DOZING GNARL

When we would visit my wife's parents, we'd travel by plane, so our son has flown frequently since he was born. Even so, he's always had meltdowns in airports.

"Come on, remember!" I'd tell him.

"You remember, don't you?" my wife would prompt.

For some reason, those words worked magic. Early on, when the only word he could say was "Mama," it's doubtful that he understood. Even so, he would respond. His head, buried in my wife's neck, would stop its frantic shaking. His eyes would darken, as if searching for the form of the words—though for him they were not words but sounds—that might be floating in the air. He'd have a faraway look in his eyes, as if recalling those trips through the sky he'd taken while in his mother's womb. It's a look unique to babies, as if they have leaped outside the bounds of gravity and time—or rather, a look that transports others outside those bounds.

But that day, no matter how I urged him to remember, it was no good. We had taken his mother to her parents'

house in our home country to have the baby, and he and I were on our way back to the house at the edge of the woods. He wouldn't stop crying. His voice resonated in the vaulted hall of the newly built terminal. To the people about to board airplanes, the sound of my son wailing with enough force to shake the cluster of abstract objects hanging from above may have seemed an ill omen. I personally would prefer not to hear a sound like that before a flight. In that ultramodern airport where the discord of emotion—the sadness of parting, the joy of reunion—seemed merely one of many functions comprising the whole, my son's animalistic screams were jarringly out of place. I felt uncomfortable, as if I were being censured not only by the people scurrying past and casting nervous glances our way, but by the airport itself.

My son's protests were so vehement that I had to pick him up and carry him. He wriggled and squirmed with no apparent fear of falling. As we approached the gate, his shrieks of "No!" were enough to break the eardrums, and the hearts, of everyone in earshot. He arched his back, kicked wildly, and scratched me on the face. Anyone seeing us would have taken me for a kidnapper. I sensed that people were lingering to watch. I glanced at a nearby security guard; he was holding his walkie-talkie to his mouth and looking at me with narrowed, suspicious eyes. At the entrance to the gate, I had to turn back.

My son kept on sobbing, but his flailing stopped. With his arms tight around my neck, he gripped my jacket, trembling.

The woman at the counter where I had checked my bag before quickly sized up the situation. There wasn't much time before takeoff, but without the slightest sign of annoyance she efficiently took care of the necessary procedures. My son's face, swollen from crying, eloquently said all that needed to be said. There would be, however, no refund.

"We won't get on the airplane. It's okay. We won't go by airplane." I had to say this over and over until he calmed down. Even then, he kept shrieking "No!" so often that I felt like slapping him. Knowing myself capable of such rage only made me more depressed.

He went on breathing hard for a while. In between shuddery breaths these words came and went: "G-go home...h-home...go hooome...home."

"Right. Let's go back and see Mommy." I had no choice but to return to my in-laws' house. What had been the point of all that frantic, last-minute packing?

I tried to pick him up, but he said he would walk. "Want to hold hands?" I asked. He shook his head. I pushed a cart loaded with the suitcases and headed for the airport bus terminal. He followed behind. Along the way, I had to look back again and again to make sure that he was still following. After we got on the bus, he didn't say another word. For a while there was hiccupping and sniffling, and then all sounds vanished. His limbs went slack, and he slept. His hair was plastered to his forehead with sweat.

Maybe I should have left him with her. Her parents said he was welcome to stay as long as he liked.

It was my wife who told me to take him back to the house at the edge of the woods. He had just started getting used to the language, so it would be a shame to keep him away, she had said. "You can manage him by yourself, can't you? You work at home anyway, so you can look after him fine."

But I knew he would miss her and go into hysterics. I would have to listen to his heartrending cries for his mother; I would feel awful, tortured with guilt. I put up a fight, going on about damage to a child's psychological development caused by separation from the mother at this stage. My wife was unyielding.

"You and Daddy can live together for a while, right?" she said to him. "Right?" Anxiety made his eyes as moist as soft-boiled egg yolks, and she knew it, but she gave that word "Right?" a little emphasis, as if to erase his anxiety. "Just for a little while. Mommy will be home soon with the baby, so you'll be fine, okay?"

He always made a great effort to put his best foot forward around her; he could hardly say no. If he had said straight out that he didn't want to live with me, I would not have been very happy. So, when he nodded, moving his head up and down as if banging it on something, he may have had my feelings in mind.

"Are you really going back?" my brother-in-law asked.

"Yes." I gave a firm nod. My brother-in-law is a giant over six and a half feet tall, so when I talk to him my chin tends to be up in the air, and I nod with needless exaggeration. As if fervently agreeing with everything he says. My son loves to ride on the shoulders of his big uncle. Both of my wife's parents are taller than me, too. In that family of giants, the only one shorter than me is my wife.

My brother-in-law bent down and asked, "When?"

"Next Thursday, I think. Why?"

He glanced at my son, who was draped on his mother and chattering away. "I promised him I'd take him to the aquarium."

"Oh, you did? Thanks so much."

"He says he wants to see the dolphins."

"No kidding. He said that?" I was a little surprised.

"A baby dolphin was born." His voice floated as gently as light on the surface of the sea, seen from underwater.

"A baby?"

"Yes." He nodded over my head. "A dolphin there gave birth recently."

"Huh."

"But we have to go soon."

"Why's that?" I looked up. I could see his chin.

"Baby dolphins don't live long in an aquarium."

"They don't?"

"Apparently not. I don't really know. But I'd like him to see the baby while it's still alive."

"There might not be many more chances."

My brother-in-law used to be a government worker in the Kinki region, but several years ago, he decided to take over the small engineering firm run by his aunt and uncle, so he quit his job and returned to his hometown. The aunt and uncle, who live near his parents, are childless and treat him and my wife like their own children. They dote on our son, their grandnephew, like grandparents.

It had seemed to me the boy would be far better off staying with his mother in this environment. He was crazy about *Bob the Builder*, a TV show featuring construction trucks and other heavy equipment as protagonists. When his great-uncle found this out, he took him to his firm's office. The empty lot that served as company parking was lined with power shovels, bulldozers, dump trucks, and cement mixers.

"Lookit those! Lookit, Daddy!" my son shouted, pulling my hand. His eyes danced with joy.

Seeing what had him so excited, his great-uncle grinned wryly. "No, no, little one. Those aren't ours."

Alongside the other trucks were several cement mixers from the ready-mixed concrete plant his cousin ran. My son looked up at him with a woebegone face.

"Wait just a minute." His great-uncle, who loved children, stuck his hand in his work pants pocket to retrieve his phone. "I'll ask if we can borrow one. Business is bad, so he's not using them all. I heard some of his drivers have had to go on leave."

"Wait," I interrupted as he was starting to place the call. "I don't think I can drive a cement mixer."

"Sure you can." With his free hand he slapped me on the shoulder with the sound a green woodpecker makes as it drills a hole in a tree. "Cement mixers are all automatics now. Even I can drive them. In the old days, they didn't even have power steering. They were the devil to steer."

"I didn't mean that," I was forced to say. "The thing is, I only have a regular driver's license."

"No worries."

The sound might actually have been coming from a green woodpecker in the grove behind the office.

"It's all automatic, so anybody can drive one. You're a worrywart, aren'tcha? Junior here wants a ride, don'tcha, little fella?" He tousled my son's hair.

In the end, my son was content with my driving the cement mixer around the lot just a little. The great-uncle was right; the machinery was far easier to handle than I had expected. My son was thrilled. After we got home, that's all he talked about to his mother.

Now, to give him another thrill, my brother-in-law had borrowed a dump truck for the ride to the aquarium. The dump truck jounced, so my wife begged off.

The boy didn't mind. He could be independent and dependent at will, even more so once my wife announced the coming arrival of an intruder. Unbelievably, he went for a sleepover at his uncle and aunt's house all by himself. Had he wanted to make his mother jealous? Or was he preparing to separate from her?

In any case, while he was at his grandparents' house, he was happy.

I was concerned. Since living alone with me, my son was using fewer and fewer words, conveying his thoughts more and more through gestures and facial expressions. He seemed to be regressing into infancy. Was it because he wished to return to a time and a place when happiness was not segmented, when there was no need to understand it as such? I thought that at his grandparents' he had laughed a lot more. In the airport, he had sobbed that he wanted to go "home." But where was home? The house at the edge of the woods? Wasn't the other place much homier to him? But no, I thought. His memories of the mother he was tied to—that he had once literally been tied to, in the womb—all began in the house at the edge of the woods.

My son knew perfectly well that the house at the edge of the woods was his real home. Just like his absent-minded mother (since his rival was still inside her, he had exclusive rights to the title of "just like"), he had merely forgotten. As proof, when we left his grandparents' house the second time, it was as if the uproar the first time had never occurred. Not only did he not cry, he made no show of resistance. My brother-in-law drove us to the airport. Our son sat in his car seat with an unchildlike, solemn look on his face, strapped in so he couldn't move, resolved that this was the end, looking—with a serenity born of the knowledge that he would be reunited with his loved one in the world to come—heroic. The small hero looked earnestly into the face of his mother, bending over him with difficulty due to her unwieldy belly.

"Mommy will be coming home soon, too. Be a good boy and listen to Daddy."

She kissed him on the forehead and cheeks. Maybe that was the magic. No sooner did we start the car than he was fast asleep. It seemed a shame to wake him up, so my brother-in-law carried him all the way into the airport. As he showed no sign of waking, I borrowed a stroller at the ticket counter. Even on the airplane, he slept soundly. "Do you have to go pee?" Along the way I woke him several times to ask, but each time, with eyes so unfocused I couldn't be sure if he was looking at me or not, he shook his head, then curled into a ball, snuggling back under the blanket like a puppy burrowing under its mother, and went back to sleep. That's how he tried to recapture it—the travel experience he had known inside the dark waters within his mother, not once awakening or being disturbed by a nuisance like me. Which must be why, later, when I asked him about it, he looked at me blankly.

"You must have been really tired. You never woke up, so I got worried. You were like a sleeping prince. But my kisses never woke you up. I guess Daddy's kisses won't do."

I laughed, but he never cracked a smile. No matter how I explained, he didn't remember. Just as no one can remember what it's like in the womb.

In any case, he stayed asleep till we arrived at the house at the edge of the woods. After we landed at the airport, I had to ask an agent to lend me a stroller. Seeing that my hands were full, without my asking, she kindly pushed the luggage cart all the way to the parking lot. From the airport to the edge of the woods, I avoided the highway and took the national road instead. I have never liked driving very much and hardly go anywhere by car unless necessary. I would have preferred not to drive home from the airport if possible. Behind the hill where the shopping mall towers like a castle is a station where the express train to the airport makes a stop. The station is a thirty-minute drive from home. All things being equal, I would have preferred to take the express train, but finding long-term parking is problematic and after a trip abroad there is always extra luggage. Too often I end up going to and from the airport by car.

After we returned, I had to take my son to that railway station nearly every day. He loved the show *Thomas & Friends*, but of course trains weren't why he wanted to go to the station. I concocted all manner of excuses why we couldn't go, but he'd cried so hard that he went into seizures, and I feared that not only his body but his very soul would come apart. The knot of my resolution easily dissolved.

"I'm going to meet Mommy," he'd announce, his eyes as bright and clear as the air after rain.

We'd stand in the large hall that was the waiting room, watching the train approach. The train would come to a stop and the doors open. Passengers spewed out, pouring into the hall, while my son waited with bated breath. The sounds and colors filling the hall merged with our memories, expanding until they formed a turbulent river that bore us far from the image of what mattered most. Day after day, we saw no trace of the person we were hoping for.

"She's not here..." Tired of waiting, he'd look ready to cry.

I would pretend to dial my phone. "Gee, that's funny, no answer," I'd say and shake my head. Or pretend the phone in my pocket was vibrating and act surprised.

"Is it Mommy?" His voice still radiated light, but day by day the shadow of doubt was deepening.

I would crouch down and show him a text message he couldn't read. "She says she missed the train," I'd say. "What a scatterbrain!"

"Yeah," he would agree, his head tilted as if to rid his body of doubt.

Then I would launch into a convincing explanation of just how scatterbrained Mommy was. "Remember that time when Daddy's CD case got broken? That was because Mommy stepped on it and broke it."

It was curious how often things disappeared from the house at the edge of the woods. I still hadn't found the copy of *The Origin of Species* I'd been reading before bed. When lost things didn't turn up, my wife always blamed it on the woods. "The imps and animals and birds who live in the woods are playing tricks on us," she'd say.

Maybe that's why I got the urge to listen to Ravel's fantasy opera *L'enfant et les sortilèges*. The day I bought the CD, my wife, who'd been vacuuming, rushed to answer the phone and stepped on the case, cracking it but good (it was a long call, so she never did finish the vacuuming). The cracked case then slid under the bed, and later when I found it and opened it, it was empty. Before my wife left she had stuck her favorite CDs, those she thought would be good for the baby's development, in a CD carrier to take with her, so maybe the Ravel was in that stack. Or maybe she had mislaid it somewhere. After all, she had left without even taking her phone. In any case, I knew that CD wasn't going to turn up.

"I wonder if she'll be there tomorrow..." my son murmured, again and again. Was he seeking an answer from me?

After a while the questions tapered off. I imagined he was getting tired of playing the role of a child who naively believes his mother is coming home.

"She'll be there tomorrow for sure," I volunteered. Watching my son in the rearview mirror, scared by his deepening silence, I started answering the question without being asked. I repeated my assurance. How many times did this make? "Yeah, tomorrow she'll be there for sure."

But for both my wife and for us, tomorrow gradually

receded. One day I realized he had stopped asking to be taken to the station.

During that time, as I drove back and forth to the station—each of us sunk in thoughts that darkened faster than the steadily lengthening night—did I see scenery that resembled a road? Or did my eyes also see what he saw in the dreams he had as he slept as if dead, frustrated at something unknown—since he did not yet know a word like "despair" that could serve as a receptacle—rising from the recesses of his body that was so weary of waiting, and filling him like water, without malice or goodwill, but making it hard to breathe?

At first, he saw people walking on the side of the road intermittently. Then, like a dotted line filling in, the stream became continuous and thick. Under their feet was mud. Some wore no shoes. There was an occasional donkey or cow, but they were beasts of burden, not for riding, bony and thin yet piled high with household goods. Men were bent under the weight of baskets and duffel bags that they, like the beasts, bore on their backs. Women with infants strapped to their backs or folded into the crooks of their arms gripped belongings or held the hands of children old enough to walk. Those children, too, bore bags on their backs and held the hands of younger siblings that clutched bundles and baskets. No one's hands were free. Pregnant women walked awkwardly with their bellies protruding.

How could I offer rides to everyone in this caravan?

Impossible. Yet, overcome by the sight, I pulled over, and we got out. My son said nothing. He held his breath and stared at the people with eyes of fear.

The people in the caravan didn't stop, but clearly not because we didn't exist for them. They cast glances our way, but their eyes were empty of emotion, their heads moving like blades of grass lifted by a passing breeze only to droop again.

As we stood motionless beside the car, the caravan moved forward, like misaligned time that continued to flow. Or perhaps it was we, my son and I, who were trapped in misaligned time.

I tried to speak to them, but they couldn't understand me. Perhaps they were pretending not to understand—were somehow being forced to make that sort of pretense. But who would be forcing them? Or were they acting that way of their own accord?

My son clutched my trousers, shivering. He seemed on the verge of collapsing in tears. I picked him up and held him close. I was the one clinging to him. "Let's go home," I whispered.

But hearing myself say this stunned me—for so naturally being able to believe we had a home to go to. And for saying it under these conditions, with such ease.

Sometimes I had the urge to run away, though where could I run to? Perhaps it was that feeling that had caused me to stumble, lost, into this world riddled with masses of people so disconsolate. Yet I was not lost. I alone was not lost. I still had a home to go to. These people no longer had a home and were forced to wander, lost, forever. They had been promised nothing—or were fleeing because of broken promises. Among people thus betrayed, I was now breaking a promise. In my case, to run away was to renege on a promise.

Perhaps because he was absorbed in the scene before him, my son did not return my embrace. I didn't mind. To keep from running away, I needed to be tied to him. I squeezed him tight, and he wriggled uncomfortably.

In the car, I fastened him securely in the car seat behind the driver's seat. He sat still, as if resigned, his eyes shut. I listened to his breathing like someone whose lack of sight heightened their sensitivity to sound.

As the caravan went on, the cloud cover grew patchy, like a false veil. I got the sense that it could be ripped apart at any moment and the dark red night would come pouring through, carrying all of us—these people walking at the side of the road, my son, me—to some far-off, quiet place.

There was no traffic on the road, my car being the only exception. Yet not one person in the caravan walked on the asphalt, which, despite its cracks, would surely have been far easier going than the muddy, weed-grown area alongside. The livestock remained faithful to their masters and never broke the line.

With their burdens piled high, the people were grotesque, scarcely human. As they made their way, exhausted, they kept close together, surely not only to keep from falling over. But for whose sake were they leaving the road unstepped on? Would they ever get what they coveted?

Any rain had stopped quite some time earlier, and the asphalt had dried. Puddles remained alongside the road, though, and the legions of feet tramping through them sent liquid coursing onto the road–black snakes crossing the highway.

Finally the woods came into view. I had passed through the woods many times, always by this same road, but I didn't have a clear sense of their size. It would have been the same to say that we had a little farther to go or a long way.

As I speeded up, the trees on either side, dense with foliage, gave the impression they were falling toward us, one after another. It was the same everywhere, and just the sight of the trees made me queasy. Before long my son said he felt sick to his stomach, and I had to pull over.

The last time my wife and son and I had taken this road we'd been on our way to the airport to fly back to our home country, and the drive had taken a very long time. That's because our son had gotten carsick, worse than ever before. He turned pale and moaned that his stomach hurt. Time and again I had to pull over.

He would bend double at the foot of a tree and vomit. Even when there was nothing left in his stomach, he was racked by pain, making pitiful retching sounds.

Our son's whimpering and retching formed a natural counterpoint to the countless sounds that filled the woods. As happens in a concert hall after the conductor and musicians have taken the stage, the murmur swelled momentarily, followed by a more perfect silence. And then the performance began. Sounds slipped between the leaves and enveloped our poor son. The twitter of birds soothed his nerves. Our sense of time and distance blurred. The cries of the birds and the sighing of wind in the grasses led us to a faraway place that we could not identify by name. Then, the unexpected silences amid the floating panoply of sounds would awaken us. And we would realize that we had not moved a step.

The woods were an enormous, mysterious orchestra that played musical fragments, never revealing the piece in its entirety, a piece that seemed endless. The light, the breeze, the birdsong, the shifting shadows–they were not the soloists. The soloists were my wife's hands, gently rubbing our son's back. As if hesitant to move forward through time, her hands slid back and forth.

Perhaps all along he had simply wanted his mother's hands. Wanted to reclaim them from the unborn baby. Those hands that lovingly stroked her round, protruding belly. Before, if he'd said he felt sick, those hands would unfailingly remove him from the car seat and hold him to her breast. Now his place was taken up by her large belly. The belly intimidated him. Even when he lay with his head in her lap, his body stiff and his eyes squeezed shut in pain, the pressure of its insistent reality never lessened against his cheek.

I took to telling him not to play in the woods. I was firm. He paid no attention. Still, I couldn't tie him to a table leg, and there wasn't any specific danger that required special alertness.

Nor had any of the stories I made up to simultaneously threaten and amuse him come to pass—the stories about imps in the woods that stole children and ate them, or a path that would lead him away, never to return, or singing that would make him lose his memory and never remember Mommy again.

Then why couldn't he go into the woods? What was the danger?

Watching TV, I didn't really get what was happening. It was as if my linguistic ability had decamped. The satellite antenna made it possible to tune into programs in multiple languages, but they all sounded equally remote and unapproachable.

My son didn't seem to mind that he couldn't understand the language spoken on the TV. Kiddie programming was the same no matter what country it was produced in: sing together, dance together, make things together, be astonished together, laugh together.

Similarly, the images on the news programs from different countries all looked the same. Black smoke rose and buildings collapsed. People, too, seemed on the point of collapse. Mothers sobbed or wailed; children bawled, teary-eyed; despair etched irreparable cracks in the faces of the old. There was no need to understand the words.

I switched channels as if searching for a message aimed at me personally. My wife was always losing or forgetting things. Maybe she'd carelessly let some of them slip onto the airwaves or screen images, and I could find them there. Things that have gone missing often turn up unexpectedly, like memories that come flooding back the moment you cease racking your brain in search of them, but the things my wife loses, once gone, are never seen again. For her to lose track of herself and go missing was beyond scatterbrained and just the sort of thing she would do, but this one time I wanted it to be different: I wanted her to turn up all of a sudden, unchanged, as if she'd never been away at all.

But the things we want we don't always get.

Or perhaps everything, the things I wanted without knowing and the things I consciously fled, were all as chaotic as reality and they all did appear before me, intact, only I was too distracted to notice.

I felt as if I were living in a peculiar abyss of time and place.

When was that? One time my son came home from the woods leading an old woman by the hand. She was wearing only a kind of bathrobe, with one breast exposed. She peed while sitting on my kitchen chair, and while I was off buying her some diapers, she vanished. But when I asked my son about her, he looked blank, claiming he knew nothing about an old woman like that.

Deep in the woods is a place that the locals continue to call "the castle." The old woman might have snuck out of there, I dimly thought. I had no grounds for thinking so. There was nothing to connect her with the castle–the former residence of the lords who ruled this area centuries ago. According to the farmer who owned the land where we lived, during the war it had been used as headquarters for the Resistance.

The woods nurtured a luxuriant growth of words. They were perfectly ordinary woods, and perhaps that's why they were less apt to provide encounters with rare fruits, nuts, or flowers than with outlandish tales and episodes. It wasn't even necessary to set foot in the woods. Rain could not extinguish the bits of greenery carried on the wind like sparks from a conflagration. The sparks became flickering green flames that burned bright, devouring the soft black earth that generations had tilled, thus fattening and increasing the woods. Along the border with human civilization, where the woods intersected with humanity, all sorts of stories flew around, whether contained in green sparks or in hot spittle. People tossed things there. What things? Things that landed with a thud, that appeared to be bodies enveloped in green flames. But they were not human. Or perhaps in a sense they were indeed human: they were leftover words, words of no consequence. Their ashes floated by, unnoticed. But a curiosity-monger could always be counted on to gather them and make a point of sharing them.

I learned local stories from the young letter carrier who came every day on his rounds. I call him young, but he could easily have been either a mature fifteen-year-old or a fifty-year-old with a boyish air. He was as thin as could be. His uniform was too big for him; with his every movement, the material appeared ready to swallow him. I doubted that his yellow plaid trousers were part of his uniform, though. The hems were ragged and frayed. Hanging from his shoulder was a leather bag stuffed with mail, so full it must have been painful to carry. He always wore a helmet of the sort skateboarders use, secured under the chin. This looked less like it was protecting his head than gnawing on it. Despite the helmet, he was always on foot.

He never had any mail for us. At least, the letter we longed to get didn't arrive. Nor was it likely to, since my wife was a terrible correspondent. When she and I traveled, the task of writing postcards always fell to me. If my son asked, that was what I planned to tell him. I figured that would satisfy him. No explanation was ever needed, though. He couldn't read, even though when his mother read to him she always tried to teach him the alphabet. In any case, there was no chance of a letter arriving that contained words I would want to read aloud to my son, so it really didn't matter whether the letter carrier was on the level or not.

All he delivered were words that did not adhere to the symbols on the page. He was a talker, and the spirits of words waiting to be given voice formed a cloud of flies that followed him everywhere. When he spoke, he waved his hands as if to drive off the flies. But the word spirits, unintimidated, would take over his soft, wet tongue. Even when he wasn't speaking, his lips, tightly closed, twitched and quivered; we could almost hear the fierce struggle within him as the profusion of word spirits fought over the limited supply of moments and shapes. Surely not every single word thus formed could be a lie.

Sometimes mysterious sounds came from the woods. At first it was a sort of coughing, nothing more, that began sometime after eleven p.m. and went on until around two in the morning. Gradually other sounds mixed in, and I heard them all the time: strained laughter escaping through rifts in existence; peculiar screams suggesting a struggle to escape the self; words that didn't seem to be words, always in the exact same cadence.

When I first came, I found the presence of these unreal sounds astonishing and frightening. That's because as time passed, they came to sound as if they were emanating from me. It was as if the memory of all the sounds made by the world and humanity had been contained in my amniotic fluid. Vibrations in that fluid had etched the memory of sound into my unborn skin, a membrane that knew no dryness, as wrinkles. Covered by smooth innocence, the grooves did not show at first, but as the years piled on and the surface of my skin wore away through exposure to sun and shadow, they appeared in intricate patterns. Passing breezes and sighs and words touched those untold grooves, widening them and freeing the sounds within. The sounds were born. No, reborn, resurrected. Like strong young shoots that crack the earth's hard crust to sprout, they unfurled new leaves, absorbing heat and light and moisture in their tiny palms, and all the sounds in the world in their small membranes. That vegetation grew and flourished, becoming, perhaps, the woods. And so, just as I was part of the woods, the woods were also part of me.

The enigmatic sounds coming from the woods made me anxious, but at the same time they also evoked dreams like those that rise from somewhere deep within you when you are absorbed in wonderful music. But dreams are dreams precisely because they are so easily awakened from. As I talked to the letter carrier and the people living around us, I realized that they had explanations (so they thought) for all of the inexplicable phenomena that they encountered around the woods.

For example, the disappearance of various things from houses around the woods—loose change, chickens, now and then a beloved wife or husband or child—was attributed entirely to the mischief of the imps who inhabited the woods. The imps were portrayed differently depending on the nature of the lost item, fitted now with the masks of child-devouring devils, now with the robes of gracious spirits who free the aged and infirm from their suffering. The imps must have found it annoying to have their identity decided by human convenience.

Was that why they reworked their plans and came up with a counteroffensive?

Was what we heard the war cry of a legion of imps on the march through the woods? Were they bent on expelling us, the human colonists who had stolen their land?

"No way." My wife laughed. She addressed her belly, which was just starting to show. "Daddy's pretty superstitious, isn't he?"

"You got me." I laughed, too. "Chalk it up to the awesome power of place."

"Awesome," she repeated.

"But what *is* it? That funny sound." It was coming slowly closer.

"Let's go see." She took me by the hand.

"Yeah, but..." I held back. "Isn't it dangerous?"

She looked back at me, eyes widened in surprise, and laid her other hand on her belly. "Whatever happens, if the three of us join forces, we'll be fine, won't we?"

She pulled my hand and laid it on her belly.

She was right. There was no danger at all. Those walking among the trees fifty of a hundred feet away were not imps.

But who saw that scene?

Was it me, with one hand laid on my wife's belly? Was it my wife, holding my hand? Or was it the child inside her, binding us together? My wife and I, and our unborn child, watched silently as the line of people stretched out before our eyes, extending beyond our range of vision to the right and left. I can't imagine how long the line was.

I wanted to avert my eyes, and I wanted my wife to avert her eyes, too. Perhaps what she saw would somehow affect the child in her womb, causing it some dreadfully sad pain and leaving an indelible scar. For a moment, that stunningly irrational thought crossed my mind. And I was afraid.

I knew very well that it was not the power of the land that had infected me with superstition. I had already been invaded to the marrow with distorted thinking. No matter how often I closed my eyes and turned my face away, reality did not vanish. Just as the line of people moving forward (although since the line never broke, it was hard to be sure it was really moving) was present here and now, so, I had no doubt, were the imps.

Coming around, I interrupted the garrulous letter carrier.

"Never mind that. You know, it seems like we're not getting our mail all the time."

Why did I say a thing like that? I may have wanted to convey that I saw him as a letter carrier. He looked at me in surprise, further widening his googly eyes. But there was something fake about his response.

"Really?"

"Absolutely."

I looked up at him. It occurred to me that each time we met, I had to look higher to see his face. Either he was still growing or I was getting shorter. But my sense of time and space was now so skewed that it really didn't matter. I continued:

"Letters that should have gotten here a long time ago still haven't arrived." Having once taken on this role, I had to play it out. "Lots of them. Isn't that odd?"

He laughed. The corners of his lips jerked up, exactly as if someone were pulling strings attached to them. His teeth were big, sharply tapered canines, and every time he opened his mouth, they came popping out of his gums. The pointed teeth were constantly changing length. Their number didn't appear to be constant, either. Sometimes I could see row upon row of teeth, as in a shark's mouth, and other times his gums were as smooth as a baby's. I didn't think my eyes were playing tricks on me. I had no doubt the teeth could change shape freely, like the eye-stalks of a snail. As he reported local gossip, a chilling smile always played about his lips. But I had never heard him talk about anything else, so maybe that was just how he looked.

"Letters from your dear wife?"

I glanced around. My son wasn't back from the woods yet.

"She must've written something she didn't want you seeing."

I was silent.

The letter carrier hitched his shoulders with glee and went on, his yellowed teeth swaying: "Or are they smokin' hot letters from a lover?" His shoulders swayed as he laughed. His teeth popped and made clinking sounds like glasses tapping for a toast.

"All right now." In my exasperation, I laughed, too.

The letter carrier's laughter went overboard and turned into a coughing spell. He was struck by such a fit of coughing that his ribs seemed about to break right through his big baggy shirt. I was afraid he was going to spit out every tooth in his mouth.

"Are you all right?"

He was crouched over with his knees bent and a hand on his chest, wheezing and gasping. I peered into his face. In time with his broken gasps, his pointy teeth moved in and out of his upper and lower gums, colliding with a sharp *clang* like the clashing of swords.

He jumped up as if nothing had happened, forcefully wiped a line of spit from the edge of his mouth, and said, as if to preempt my question, "It's 'cause of the imps."

"Wha–?" His face was a short distance away. The tips of his protruding canines were red and wet. When he'd wiped his face, he must have torn the back of his hand. The tone of his voice was serious, but that twisted smile of his kept playing about his lips.

"The reason the letters disappear. It's 'cause of the imps. Better keep a close eye on your mailbox. It's not only you with missing mail, you know. Happens all the time around here, always has. They're suckers for the written word, you could say. Big readers."

"They?"

"The imps."

"They read people's mail? Without asking?"

"Why steal it otherwise? To wipe their asses?" The letter carrier burst out laughing. His laughter was so contagious, I joined in.

"Might be an improvement over leaves at that." After taking a breath, I composed my features into a solemn expression and shook my head. It wouldn't do to have him laugh so hard he suffered another coughing fit. "No, but really. That's not the point. You're saying that imps steal letters and read them? Is that right?"

"Whaddaya think? You think they deliver them out of the kindness of their hearts?" In a high-pitched voice, he said, "Registered mail! Sign here, Donald! Okay! *Quack quack quack!*" Then, returning to his normal voice, he said bitingly, "This is no Disney cartoon, you know. If they did that, I'd be out of a job! And then what would happen to me?" His lip rolled up, and the teeth that popped out of his dry, purple gums trembled furiously. "What happens to us?"

"Us?" I swallowed the rest of my words.

"Yeah, man. What happens to us?"

Startled by the sudden hatred in his large eyes, I could not speak.

"Why're they still here? Why can't we wipe 'em out?

Vermin. Vermin. They're vermin, I tell you! Why doesn't anybody speak up? They're still here, I tell you! The woods are crawling with them, I tell you! They're dangerous, I tell you! Why doesn't anybody do anything? It's more than the mail. They're trying to steal the inside of our heads! Doesn't matter how carefully I deliver the mail, I tell you! How can we just let it go? How can we?"

When it was the time the letter carrier usually came around, to avoid talking to him I made a habit of going for a walk in the woods with my son. When we came back I would check the mailbox, but it was always empty. It didn't matter whether imps from the woods had stolen them or whether the letter carrier, figuring the imps were just going to steal them and read them anyway, had ripped them up and thrown them away: there were no letters.

On windy days, countless shreds of paper danced like fragments of words that had lost all meaning forever. The dry blizzard danced around us. Whittled by the cold, sharp wind and kneaded by the faint light, the whirling shreds gradually taking the shape of a woman...no, that could never happen.

My heart ached. I clasped my son to my chest, pressed my cheek against his, and held him tight. He submitted silently to my embrace and, casting his troubled gaze on the fluttering cascade of paper shreds, endured the self-indulgent behavior of his suddenly sentimental father.

Various things began to disappear. I realized that food was missing from the refrigerator. I knew my son had taken ham and sausage, yogurt and cheese, milk and orange juice. Did he do it knowing that I was onto him?

Yes, of course he did. Once he asked me to boil him an egg, even though he doesn't like eggs. Then who would eat the egg he took? The letter carrier had informed us that eggs were a favorite of the imps. A weakling imp would get on all fours, bottom pointed toward a still-warm egg just stolen from underneath a hen, give a backward kick, and send the egg rolling against a stone or a wall to crack it open, he told us, the venom that always dripped from his words laid aside. *Are you sure you're not talking about squirrels?* I started to say, but thought better of it. I'd had more than enough of staring at the pointy teeth in his mouth coming and going as he jabbered on. All he ever delivered were unwelcome stories I didn't want to hear.

Was my son taking food out to the woods because he wanted to draw my attention to something? Then why be furtive about it? He was hiding something. There could be no doubt that he was hiding something in the woods.

Perhaps he wanted me to join him in caring for someone sheltering in the woods.

It wasn't only food that he took. Blankets and cushions disappeared, too. So did a big package of toilet paper. It was as if my son himself had become an imp.

But was he really looking after someone or something? Trying to help?

Didn't he know what was in that green plastic container?

"Where are you going with that?" I called out.

My son had just come out of the storage shed, and started with surprise. He looked up at me. The nearly full container was heavy for him.

"Are you taking that into the woods?"

He didn't answer.

"You know what that is, right?"

The object he was clutching like a big stuffed animal contained an agricultural chemical for killing tree stumps. I had bought it at the nursery in the shopping center. Although exactly the same shape as a container of laundry detergent, it was a lurid green and prominently imprinted with the word DANGER above a skull and crossbones symbol.

It had been my wife's idea to plant a flower garden in the southern part of the yard. "As a family of four, let's cultivate flowers." I had my own idea, which was to plant a tree of some kind for the child on the way.

"What if the tree dies?" She sounded appalled. "I would have thought you'd learned your lesson."

When our son was born, I bought a fir tree less than a year old and planted it in a corner of the yard with the idea that he and the tree could grow up together. The following year's extreme heat quickly did in the sapling. We had not told our son any of this, of course.

"You're pretty superstitious yourself, no?" I said.

"Not as much as you. And this time if the tree died, we wouldn't be able to keep it a secret. Even if you and I said nothing, this little guy would spill the beans to his sister." She looked down at our son, who was wound around her thigh.

We had just heard from the maternity clinic that our next child would be a girl. Our son had been clingy since right before my wife found out she was pregnant. Of course he could be petulant, too, sometimes contrary. Perhaps he instinctively sensed the presence of a rival, even before his mother knew. In any case, he almost never left her alone. As if mere physical proximity was not enough to allay his fears, he spun words and sighs into an unbroken thread that he wrapped around her constantly. He was willful, demanding, and whiny, seeking to monopolize her attention.

"You'd tell her everything, wouldn't you? Meanie."

He had no idea what she was talking about, but he looked up at her and said, "Yeah" in a strong, happy voice.

In the end, we decided to create a flower garden, just as my wife had suggested. The former resident had planted a lot of trees in the yard. I had no intention of cutting down the fruit trees—apricot, plum, apple. We decided to convert the unused area along the south side to a flower bed. Not wanting to taint the soil, we would have preferred not to use strong chemicals to kill the tree roots, but there was one tree in the proposed site that I simply couldn't dig out. There was no choice. I took a saw to it, close to the roots, and felled it. Then I bought a white powder to kill the stump and roots.

I put on a pair of thick gardening gloves and rubbed the powder into the stump. I dug around the roots, sprinkling powder into the ground, and covered it over with soil so it wouldn't fly away in the wind. My son, watching from close by, wanted to help. The container wouldn't open unless you pushed down hard while turning the cap. He lacked the strength and skill to do that, but the cap was already off. He grabbed the container and tipped it, holding out his hand to catch the powder.

"No!" I shouted. In a stern tone I added threateningly, "You'll die."

Quickly he let go of the container, turned to it and, copying my gesture, wagged a finger as he yelled, "No!"

I laughed. "Who are you trying to fool?"

Seeing me laugh, he laughed back in seeming relief—or maybe he was just drawn in despite himself.

So he must know that the green container held a dangerous chemical. Could he have forgotten? In the meantime, he kept snatching food from the house and carrying it into the woods.

He must be trying to save someone. To help them.

Are there situations in which giving someone a deadly poison would save them?

Whom or what was my son trying to save?

I didn't believe that Battu, who could barely walk straight, could possibly survive in the woods.

Battu was the dog we had gotten from the humane society in the neighboring town. The idea was simple: I hoped that getting a dog might relieve in some measure the vast emptiness in the house.

I never imagined that there could be so many abused animals in this small country. In the building of the humane society, the office, corridor, and courtyard were full of caged animals. Often there were several animals to a cage, mostly dogs and cats, each huddled in a corner.

"We have to cage them like that," said a female employee. "If we let them out, there'd be pee and poo everywhere."

In fact, the place was enveloped in the rank smells of excrement, urine, and unwashed animals.

The woman was tremendously fat. Her trousers were stretched tight, bulging over the sides of her chair. Though the room was on the chilly side, she was wearing a king-size white T-shirt—dingy and stained—printed with the organization's logo. Her bare arms were like logs, with a red rash at the elbows.

My attention was drawn to her breasts. So monumental that each of them could have held an unborn child, they hung down over the many folds of her mounting stomach. What really surprised me was the sudden appearance, poking out from between those pendulous globes, of a pair of little heads. The two squirrels instantly scampered to the top of the woman's head, which was covered with chestnut hair as unkempt as if she'd just gotten out of bed. The squirrels' heads with their pointed ears leaned down as one reached toward her right eye, the other her left. Perhaps to maintain their balance as they hung upside down, their large fluffy tails stuck up from the woman's head, swaying like a pair of antennae. The area around her eyes was purplish and swollen, as if she'd been the victim of violence. The squirrels stuck tiny fingers under her eyelids and tried to pry them open, looking perhaps for hidden food, but the eyelids were heavy and wouldn't turn up. Then suddenly, as if her bottom had been pricked with a pin, the woman moved slightly. Her lids finally opened, revealing the bloodshot whites of her eyes. The squirrels let go of the lids and slid down from her shoulders to burrow again beneath her breasts. Without realizing it, I pinched and pulled on my own belly flab.

I looked at my son. He didn't seem to have noticed the squirrels that had emerged from the woman's body. He was staring at a pile of cages by the window. In the bottom cage, cowering, was Battu.

Battu was a small mixed breed. His previous owner had been a woman in our village who used to teach in the elementary school. It wasn't the obese woman who told us her identity. As usual with such organizations, it was against the rules for them to divulge such information. Asking doesn't get you anywhere. It was the letter carrier who told us. The schoolteacher hadn't retired because she'd reached the mandatory age for retirement, he said; she'd been forced from her job. The way she treated her dog—Battu—just proved the kind of person she was.

The neighbors had noticed a constant stream of pitiful screams coming from the teacher's house. As her big yard was enclosed by a high stone wall, no one knew what might be going on inside. The house had been left to her by her lover, a conservative councilman from a respected family. After the councilman died, a man who'd been arrested for some crime—drug dealing? human trafficking? both?—moved in with her and proceeded to abuse her daily. Annoyed by the talk going around town, he hired three youths to help him smash the neighbors' cars with bats and hammers, reducing them to scrap. This they did in broad daylight, while everyone watched. And then he disappeared.

So the heartrending screams coming from the schoolteacher's house weren't from the woman herself. Unsettling though the screams were, the neighbors stayed away. Her behavior at school was disturbing enough. She'd been forced out because of discriminatory remarks she'd made to immigrant children in the classroom. My wife, learning this, was even more indignant than I was, declaring that no son of ours would ever go to a school like that. Regardless, the woman found living in a place with so many foreigners intolerable, so she left our land at the edge of the woods for some utopia inhabited only by people of pure racial stock.

When curious neighbors poked into her house once she moved away, they found a small dog. Hanging from the kitchen ceiling was not a light fixture but the dog, strung up, its legs lashed together with a rope. Its tongue was lolling and handfuls of its hair had been ripped out, leaving open, bleeding wounds. Stains covered the floor. There were only a few turds amid the dark, greenish-brown diarrhea mixed with blood. Besides the smell of the dog and its shit, there was the stink of rotten meat.

The letter carrier described this to me as vividly as if he had witnessed it himself. His nose wrinkled, his lips rolled back like fleshy petals, and the upper and lower rows of pointed canines crowding his gums stirred restlessly like a dense set of stamens with, crawling over them, the legs of myriapods.

On the floor under the little dog was a broken broomstick, splattered with blood. Apparently the schoolteacher had used it to beat the defenseless animal. The screams everyone heard had been the dog's. Perhaps there is no difference in the despair and pain that people and dogs experience. Perhaps despair and pain shake the fibers of anyone's being with the same intensity and horror.

"So that's how Battu's suffering came to an end," the letter carrier said, winding up his gruesome account.

"Battu?" I said. "What's that?"

"The dog's name."

The rows of teeth kept coming and going inside his mouth, as if alive.

Every time I saw him, his physique and height were different. That day, as if my vision had been cut off by elevator doors, he appeared extremely tall and thin.

His gaze wandered, not lighting on me in particular. With fingers like insects camouflaged as twigs he scratched at his helmet, the strap tightly fastened under his chin. As usual, he was wearing yellow plaid pants. They were unusually wrinkled.

I looked at the woods behind him. The trees had shed all their leaves.

"Tell me something," I began diffidently, having long wanted to ask him this. "You know...um...are those pajama pants?"

The letter carrier responded by bending over, folding his tall, thin body in half. There was a crackling sound, like stepping on dry branches. I feared his ribs had broken.

He lifted his head up. The canine teeth swarming in his mouth burst wide open. Droplets of laughter sprayed over me, as simultaneously big drops of rain like insect eggs struck the top of his helmet.

For several days it was a constant downpour. Thunder shook the woods. We stayed indoors, spending time in front of the TV, watching the news.

Our rain was heavy, but it wasn't actually that bad, not like what we saw on the screen. There was footage of houses half-submerged in water. It wasn't clear where the flooding was. It could well have been someplace I saw every day.

Before I could tell whether it was a religious structure or merely a tall building looming over the distant townscape, blurred by the driving rain, the image changed. A road under a gray sky crisscrossed by slack power lines had become a canal. Car tires were under water, invisible. Some cars were on their side or overturned. A line of drenched people, their legs struggling against the current, crossed the canal. The camera lens, too, was wet. The world was so thoroughly saturated that if I had reached out and wiped the screen, I wouldn't have been surprised to find drops of water on my fingertips. Some people were getting around by boat.

The TV camera showed a chicken coop left behind by a family who had evacuated. Behind the chicken wire, the waters had risen high, lifting several birds almost to the ceiling. It was not clear if they were dead or alive. They seemed to be huddled together, but perhaps their cold bodies had merely been swept into a corner by the muddy torrent.

The camera then showed the interior of the house. As in the room where we sat watching, there was a television set and a sofa. But on the sofa, something was moving. The camera moved in closer and a spotlight was turned on. It was a dog, soaking wet and shivering, curled into a ball, its fur so black and frizzy, it looked singed. Even when the camera went in close, the dog didn't lift its nose, which was tucked into its body, but only stared back with frightened eyes radiating anxiety. Rather than zooming in, the camera was swallowed in the dog's small eyes. The screen began to slowly darken and dissolve.

Not only the camera but we were also drawn into the dog's eyes. The screen was the surface of a raging current pelted by endless rain. The swaying layer of water washing over everything in wrinkles and creases resembled the slack, ashen skin of starving cows and horses and—as the screen perpetually showed—human beings. The turbid current was so complete in itself that it formed an eddy of time different from that of the furiously pounding rain, blotting out the infinitesimal spaces between sounds and allowing not even the tiniest relief of silence. Water may have overflowed from the TV screen and come flooding onto the floor of the room where my son and I sat watching. Was the sound of water pouring from the trembling screen that had become the eyes of the little dog? Or did it come from beyond the windows misted over by the pelting rain? Or had it emerged from the inner recesses of existence, the far reaches of memory? Unable as we were to tell where we ourselves were located, there was no need for such distinctions.

On the way back from the humane society in the neighboring town, Battu shivered on my son's lap. His fur was, for some reason, wet. When I stroked it, my fingers came away sticky.

"Probably stress from the abuse he suffered messed up his secretory glands," the woman had said. Whether there are voices that suit fat people I don't know, but hers was melancholy—the low, somewhat raspy voice of a smoker. On her desk, amid piles of papers, was an ashtray heaped with cigarette butts. I was surprised that an employee of the humane society would smoke. The cramped office reeked of animals. I was wearing a wool coat, and when I came inside my first thought was that my coat might start to smell like that. Perhaps for her, smoking served to mask the smell.

Why my son picked Battu, I don't know. He insisted that Battu was the dog he wanted.

"Really? You want Battu? He'll never become attached to you," the woman said.

When I heard the dog's name, it came to me: this was the animal the letter carrier had been talking about. Certainly no dog so abused would ever trust humans again.

It was tough getting Battu out of his cage. The entrance was too small for the woman's thick arms. Battu pressed himself into a far corner, shaking so hard I thought he might dislocate a joint. The woman's every movement shook the cage, swaying the whole pile and giving the cats and birds in higher cages conniptions. There was no help for it; I stuck my arm in the cage. The unpleasant sensation felt less like getting hold of a dog and more like grasping an animal's viscera—alive and twitching. And Battu smelled awful, like shit and rotten garbage. Did my son really want a dog like this? I looked at him. He held out his arms with a happy smile.

"Really?" the woman asked again, taking an administrative form from her desk.

Not knowing what to do with my hands, which were covered with gunk, I spread my arms and shrugged.

"You're sure?" she pressed, handing me a pen. "The other thing is, he can't run properly. You won't be able to take him for walks."

She explained that because of the abuse Battu had suffered–she didn't go into detail, but thanks to the letter carrier I knew all about it–his ankles were permanently damaged and deformed. He could only walk on what in humans would be the tippy-toes, and with a slow dragging motion.

"That's the one he wants, so what can I do?" I said.

"But will a dog like that ease his loneliness?" she said softly. Her big, fleshy lips might have tried to smother the words, but I heard them.

I looked into her face. Between her swollen eyelids and her cheeks full to bursting, her eyes had vanished, buried in flesh. The squirrels that I had seen lift her heavy lids remained hidden under her massive breasts. Yet her reaction struck me as very reasonable. This was a small town. If something was going on in a family, something dreadful, word got out. It didn't matter that we lived at the edge of the woods, far from the center of town. After all, there was a postal worker who delivered not letters but rumors and gossip.

Instead of being strapped in his car seat, my son wanted to ride next to me in the passenger seat with Battu in his lap.

"The dog's bound to pee all over him," the woman had said, taking some newspapers from a pile on the floor and handing them to me. They smelled suspiciously of feces, though that could have been my imagination.

I spread newspapers on my son's lap and set Battu on top of them. Although the dog's coat was greasy and sticky, my son petted him happily. Battu, perhaps resigned to his unknown fate, curled himself into a tight ball, his head hidden, and lay motionless on my son's lap, though he never stopped shaking. On the way home I had to stop the car once and change the newspapers after Battu soiled them. Not only his secretory glands but his intestinal system was in bad shape. I took out some tissues and tried to wipe his behind. He wriggled, struggling to get away, so over and over I ended up having to wipe not just his anus but my own hand.

While wrapping the soiled tissues in the soiled newspaper, I glanced at the words on the page. Would it have been meaningful, or ironic, if the newspaper contained an article about the racist comments made at school by the teacher who had abused Battu? Such unexpected coincidences found in well-crafted stories do happen in real life. But nothing so surprising was written in the newspaper that I crumpled into a ball. I saw photographs of black smoke, destroyed cars and houses, ambulance crews and ordinary citizens carrying stretchers, and, visible between them, body parts. War and armed conflict showed no sign of ending. People hid their faces in their hands or grimaced, wept, or stared emptily and helplessly into space. Whether or not their mouths were open, they emitted soundless, poignant cries that anyone bothering to look could hear.

I turned on the car radio. It was time for the opera broadcast. That day, it was Mozart's *Magic Flute*, and Papageno was singing. Back when my son hadn't lost his sparkle and forgotten how to be playful, he used to summon me by singing "Pa-pa-pa-Papageno!"—no doubt imitating his mother. The voice over the car radio liberally bestowing warm vitality upon us made me glad, but at the same time I knew too much: somewhere I had read that as Mozart lay on his deathbed surrounded by his loved ones, he had asked them to sing Papageno's aria.

Battu vanished in an unguarded moment.

No, that description is inaccurate. Since Battu dragged his feet, he could not have vanished in a moment, as if snatched by a devil, spirited away by a deity, or carried off by imps. But suddenly we realized he was gone. The woman at the humane society had gone out of her way to warn that he wouldn't take to us. We were simply careless.

We always kept him inside the house.

"You never know what dangers there might be outside.

There are imps in the woods, too. So let's be careful not to let Battu out of the house." I said this in the car as my son looked up at me and nodded while petting Battu, whose shivering grew more intense the longer he was on my son's lap. My son wasn't so much stroking the dog's back as winding his hand through peculiar knobs of fur-covered flesh. And did he really nod? He and I were both panting in an exaggerated way, more than Battu. Once at the house, Battu never came within three feet of us. Trying to hold him was a circus. He would flee if approached. Even though he couldn't run in a straight line, he was good at escaping our clutches. His movements were like those of a rolling rugby ball, impossible to predict. The house was small, but my son and I chased him until we were out of breath.

Cornered, Battu would raise a pitiful howl, as if we were beating him with a broom. Being exposed to his howl made *me* want to cry. My son found it unbearable. When I'd get ahold of Battu and hand him to my son, he would clutch the dog tight to his chest and snuggle his cheek against him. The leather bag with knobs of fur would then let out a plaintive sound, like wind slicing the air. I'd get down on my hands and knees and wipe up the urine and feces on the floor.

I was outdoors, preparing the flower bed my wife had wanted: "Let's the four of us cultivate flowers." Despite the agricultural chemical I had used, the stump showed no sign of dying. Far from it: little branches with tiny green leaves were sprouting from its side. In order to kill it off once and for all, I'd dug up around the roots to expose them again and was in the process of rubbing the chemical into them thoroughly, using a bit more than the last time, when I sensed an awkward movement behind me.

"Is it really in the way?" a voice said.

"Yeah, it is," I replied to the familiar-sounding voice. "It's an eyesore, too."

"It is?"

"Yeah," I said, rubbing the white powder between the roots. "And if it uses up all the nutrition in the soil, the flowers won't bloom."

"They won't?"

The skepticism in the voice made me lose confidence. "Okay, I don't know that for sure, but they won't be as pretty."

"I don't think they have to be pretty. Maybe you should have left the tree there, too."

Now I was mad. I stood up and turned around.

No one was there. Or rather, my son was there, looking at me.

I sighed. "What's up?"

"Telephone," he said, holding out his hand. In his hand was my phone, but it wasn't ringing or vibrating.

"Who was it? Did you answer it?"

He covered his mouth with his hands as if to stifle a scream. He turned and looked at the house. The kitchen door was wide open. "Battu," he said in a small voice.

We rushed back to the house, but Battu was nowhere to be seen. He wasn't between the sofa and the wall or under the beds.

We looked around the perimeter of the house. We even went into the woods. "Battu! Battu!" Our voices resounded through the woods. Whether the ground was thickly covered with withered, decaying leaves, or whether each tree became a supersensitive sound collector, gathering words and sounds and expressing them as green leaves, I can't exactly recall. All I'm sure of is that my son did not cry and carry on.

"How many times have I told you to close the door when you go outside?"

But he never looked my way. His gaze, huge and empty out of all proportion to his small frame, hovered all about him. It was hard to believe that this was the same boy who whined and blubbered if he was scolded or reprimanded even a little. Come to think of it, he hadn't had a meltdown since that time in the airport. Could he have used up all his tears there? Was it because he had already experienced a loss so great that no accumulation of small losses could ever approximate it? Did he understand that experience as loss?

Battu isn't lost: that's how my son may have intuitively felt. No one had seen the dog die. He was in the woods, alive. As proof, all our searching never turned up his dead body.

It was soon after that, I think, that my son began taking food into the woods. For all the world as if he were setting out on a picnic, he would go into the woods wearing a backpack that I had watched him stuff with food, drinks, and his favorite books and toys. No matter how I warned him of the danger of the root-killing chemical, he kept trying to take the green container with him. In his imagination, he was an explorer or a knight in shining armor. And a hero needs a weapon. Perhaps my telling him over and over about the danger of the chemical only backfired. It was a powerful weapon able to defeat enemies. But where was there an enemy as strong as that? And whom was he trying to save?

Watching my son's back as he disappeared into the woods, I thought, *It's okay, buddy. Yeah. Battu is living happily ever after with the imps in the woods.*

At first I didn't notice the phone ringing. I peeled off the blanket and got up off the sofa, but I felt lethargic and weak-kneed. I almost fell over.

"Hello?"

All I could hear was a tone that sounded like a thread stretching to infinity, severed at regular intervals. The line had been cut off.

I sighed, wrapped the blanket around me, and sat down heavily on the sofa. Then I reached for the remote, which had fallen on the floor, to turn on the TV.

The screen wavered like the sea at night. I changed the channel, but everywhere I looked there was water. The scene was vaguely familiar. A collapsed trestle. A raging torrent slamming into support posts that had nothing to support. Apparently, the bridge had not yet been repaired.

A different scene appeared on the screen. Water, again. This time I could place it right away. I knew this scene very well. It was the river that wound through our woods. We often picnicked there. On Sunday afternoons when the weather was nice, so many people came to the riverbank and the adjacent park seeking sunlight that you'd wonder where they had been hiding in this little town. People lying down reading books, exposing as much of themselves to the sun as they dared. Couples on the grass, bodies entwined. Old people walking along holding hands, supporting each other. Scampering children. Families like ours.

The bench where we used to sit and spread out our bento was engulfed in swirling muddy water. A voice came on: "The enclosure around the lumberyard of a sawmill upstream has been destroyed in the floodwaters." I knew there was a place where timber felled in the woods was stored in the water. In the slanting rain, logs now clogged the river, knocking and grinding into each other, rising and falling with the current.

I couldn't believe my eyes. Timber was floating downriver, the narrator had said, but these were not logs, they were human beings, drowning or drowned in the lashing rain. Corpses, too many to count, wrapped in dirty, torn clothing, rags, or just lacerated skin, I couldn't tell which.

In the rushing current, stiffened limbs thrust up from the water, only to be pushed down again. Faces were impossible to make out. Mouths were half-open, gasping for breath to make a sound. Last words remained stuck in throats, unheard. Individual tragedies were swallowed by the great torrent of death.

I was thirsty. I heard the sound of rain, of flowing water. From outside the house? From the TV? I stretched out a hand toward the screen, though I was not seeking to grasp one of the innumerable hands that thrust above the water. I turned the remote toward the TV and pushed a button, switching the power off. Or I thought that's what I did, but I only changed the picture on the screen.

It was a scene from an old film. A black-and-white film. The interior of a large station. A train had just arrived. The doors of the coaches opened. A woman appeared, the collar of her coat turned up. At first her white breath concealed her face. She stepped down onto the platform and started walking purposefully. She wasn't being chased. She had the gait of someone who knows exactly where they are going. But the camera, unsure of her destination, followed her from behind, wavering as if lost. Then it overtook her and, as if deliberately trying to halt her progress, cut in front of her at an angle. Her face showed in close-up, eyes widened in surprise. I was more surprised than she.

Her face brightened. Her pace quickened. After remaining seated so long, even the slightest physical movement creates a sense of liberation. She strode forward, cutting through cold air like it was thin, transparent paper. Her backpack bounced and danced on her back. One hand pressed to a shoulder strap, she started to run. She raised the other hand and waved.

Here! Here I am!

A small child came toward her, whether walking or running it was hard to say. The child was wearing a yellow knit cap—how could I know that if the picture was black-and-white?—and overall he was plump, like a big stuffed animal moving by magic. That's it: a child touched by magic. The magic of a mother.

She fell to her knees and spread her arms wide, waiting for the child to fly into her embrace.

He threw himself at his mother, landing horizontally in her arms. With perfect confidence, as if taking a step down and flinging himself into an abyss were one and the same, he yielded his whole being to her.

She of course accepted him with *her* whole being.

The mother clasped the child and the child the mother, warm and close.

Eternity condensed in their embrace. Two bodies that had been separated, joined again as one.

The mother stood up, holding the child in her arms. They lay their cheeks together and then, forehead to forehead, looked into each other's eyes.

The child stretched out an arm, pointing. *Ah, ah, ah,* he said—or so I divined from the movement of his half-open mouth. For some reason I couldn't hear his voice. He seemed to be indicating the direction he wanted to go. *That way, that way.*

Her eyes followed the line extending from the tip of his pointing finger, which led to me.

That's right: she saw me.

She nodded to the child, a big smile playing about her lips. The same smile was on the child's lips, mirroring hers.

She began to walk, led by the pointing finger of the child clasped to her chest.

Her face and the child's grew bigger. Came closer. Came toward me.

Here. Here I am.

I spread out my arms, waiting.

Suddenly she turned, changing direction. Averted her face from mine.

No, that wasn't it. The camera had moved around to her side, that's all. Her profile, hidden by the child's head, went past me. I wanted to circle around in front of her and stop her, but I was helpless. All I could do was tag along beside her as she strode on. However I waved and shouted, trying to get her attention, she didn't look my way.

Then, *boom!* I had the impression that I had been thrust aside. I took a pratfall in front of the screen. Dazed, I looked up.

I could see the entire figure of the woman holding the child. She was looking at me, walking straight this way again.

And yet she receded into the distance. Growing smaller.

The camera was moving away from her faster than she was approaching with the child. The figures of other people in the train station crowd began to mingle with hers onscreen. She and the child coalesced indistinguishably. Her face and the child's fused into one. I no longer knew where they were. All I could see in the station on the screen was a writhing mass of bodies.

I tried to elbow my way into the crowd and was again thrust violently aside.

I was cold. The blanket had slipped and fallen to the floor. I must have fallen asleep on the sofa with the TV on. My joints ached. On the screen, heavy gray clouds lapped the earth, but my eyes were so dazzled, I had to squint. While rain continued to fall on the TV, wide beams of sunlight were pouring in through the uncurtained window, bearing the twittering of birds like leaves. Outside the window, above the woods, the sky was pale blue. The yard was full of puddles, each striving to absorb the sky and woods. It was as if the ground were scattered with mirror fragments reflecting countless worlds.

I felt myself fill with something like hope. I turned and looked at the TV, where although the sky was not blue, the rain had now stopped. But the positive mood that had arisen in my heart gave way to consternation. On the screen, there was no leisure for puddles and the world to engage in quiet mutual contemplation. The ground was hidden by squishy mud churned by legions of feet. Out of that mud there had to come a new world, one that was perhaps not filled with hope but that at least encouraged hope, even if that hope could never be fulfilled. Yet I saw people walking by the side of the road who had changed to beasts of burden covered in grotesquely shaped growths. The camera, which had at first shown the long unbroken line of people from a distance, moved in closer.

Now the people were walking toward the camera. Children holding hands with a mother or an older brother or sister stood on tiptoe, reaching toward the camera with their free hands. They put their hands on the frame of the screen as if trying to enter the world on the other side. But the camera backed away from them. Lifted in adult arms, the children chased the camera. Their faces grew larger. They were thin, with enormous eyes that peered into the camera. The screen clouded over from their breath. Small, dirty hands pushed against the lens, leaving sticky fingerprints. But then the screen changed, and the fingerprints disappeared as if they had never been there at all.

My son was apparently up already. When I went into the kitchen, there was a small bowl on the table with a spoon and the remnants of the Rice Krispies and milk he had eaten.

I was thirsty, so I opened the refrigerator to get something to drink. The shelves were practically empty. The milk and the orange juice were gone. There was no yogurt or cheese or ham. In front of the counter was a chair that he must have climbed on to open the cupboard doors. The bread and cookies were gone, too. His backpack wasn't in its usual place, stuffed into the shopping cart in the corner.

I went out into the yard. Worried, I checked the shed. Sure enough, the green plastic container was gone.

I headed for the woods, and on the way I looked over at the corner of the yard where the flower garden was going to go. Was the chemical inside that lurid green container any good at all? The stump that I had slathered with the white powder, determined to kill it, had put out even more new shoots. The slender shoots reached toward the sky with graceful strength, as if made of steel wire; at their tips were sweet, vibrant leaves of light green, quivering slightly as if communing with the light and wind.

The ground in the woods was covered with leaves. They were soaking wet and messy, as if they'd all been trampled; I had no chance of finding my son's footprints. He was too cautious, I knew, to go very far. He had never stayed in the woods so long that I became worried. I was confident he would turn up eventually. I wanted to take a moment to enjoy the nice weather we were finally having.

With the leaves all fallen, the woods were bright.

Sunlight burst joyfully through the woods. Somewhere in the distance was the buzz of animated voices. People hard at work, but having great fun. Perhaps tonight there would be a ball at the castle in the woods, and they were getting ready.

Yes, ordered by the wild and capricious lord of the castle, the imps were out gathering mushrooms and nuts. Flighty and scatterbrained and quarrelsome though they were, no matter what they got up to, the imps always made an occasion of it and had themselves a marvelous time.

That fantasy was abruptly cut short. I halted. Morning light, starved from having waited all night for dawn to break, was devouring a dead body. The rain had stopped a good while ago. Black ants had crawled out of their nest and were swarming over the body, so many that the skin appeared to move. The thing looked as if it were still alive. Yet quite some time must have passed since it had died. What had died, I had no idea. It was about the size of a baby.

Battu?

But hadn't my son been bringing food to the woods to feed Battu, who couldn't run properly?

From close by came the scuffle of wet leaves. I flinched, and I turned fearfully in the direction of the sound. Scattered over the leaves was food my son had brought from home. Half-eaten slices of bread. A package of ham. A squashed box of cookies. A milk carton with white liquid spilled from the spout.

Beyond the food was my son. He was standing straight, facing a tree.

Before I could call out to him, he spun around, but whether he saw me I don't know. He had already started running in my direction. I instinctively dropped to my knees and held out my arms to catch him, but he tore past me, stirring the wet leaves. With a cry that could have been either a wail or a shout of joy, he ran straight ahead through the woods where veils of sunlight fell in layer upon layer, heading home.

I, too, let out a cry.

A pregnant woman was sitting with her legs sticking straight out, her back against a tree. At the ends of limply dangling arms, her hands clutched leaves she had scraped up. Her face was the color of clay, and her closed eyes were so sunken that it looked as if she had pushed them into their sockets with her thumbs. Her cheekbones seemed ready to break through her taut, bloodstained skin. Her head was tipped back, as if someone had grabbed the hair at the back of her head to force a confession out of her, but from her half-opened mouth had issued not the words her inquisitor sought but strings of red froth. Her face alone gave no clue to her sex; it looked equally boyish and girlish. But she was definitely female. She had the unmistakable swollen belly of a pregnant woman. A belly that seemed like it might crush her thin body.

Her belly alone was alive. It was not part of her. Like

a beast that captures its prey, holds it down, and rips into its flesh with strong jaws, her round belly had attacked her, pushed her over, and snatched away her life. The excitement of the hunt still unabated, it was breathing hard, sending waves all through her. The underbrush around the pregnant woman was soaking from the streams of drool that poured from her belly's half-opened mouth as it sought to sink its teeth into her again.

As if seeking some escape, my eyes searched for the green container.

It couldn't be here. Impossible. My son could never have given her such a thing. I had told him over and over how dangerous it was.

Besides, I thought defiantly, the stupid chemical was no damn good. No matter how much powder I rubbed into that tree stump, it showed no sign whatsoever of dying, but put out new sprigs one after another, unfurling their tiny green leaves like whispers and welcoming the spring.

The enormous belly that had consumed the woman breathed. Protruding from the base of the tree like a huge gnarl, the belly dozed, heaving up and down.

I closed my eyes. Something danced behind my lids. I took a deep breath and opened them again. It hadn't gone away. The large belly was still there, still breathing.

The loud, cheerful murmurs were now close at hand.

I turned around, praying that when I turned back to the tree, the belly of the pregnant woman would be gone.

The weather was nice for a change. Anybody would want to go outdoors on a morning like this. And then I saw it again–the line of people crossing through the woods. It was not, I think, an illusion created by the fresh glare of sunlight, back after so long.

I couldn't make out their expressions. Everyone's head was bowed, for one thing, and anyway I couldn't properly open my eyes in the glare. Even so, I couldn't look away. The sun was swallowing the line of people, eroding the outlines of their jostling bodies. Shapes were lost; a smell like something burning and colors and sounds fused together. Individual differences dissolved until, as with a landslide, it was difficult to say whether the line was stationary or moving. A green flame danced like a leaping fish. It was the lurid green container of root-killing chemical, lifted high in the air again and again.

The little boy clutching the handle of the green container was making peculiar noises, and each time he did so, under his raised lip the row of pointed canines moved in and out. He was wearing yellow plaid pajamas and a black helmet. He reached up and pulled the goggles on top of the helmet down over his eyes. The left lens was cracked, as if a bullet had passed through it. Without stopping, he tipped the green container and poured white powder into his upturned palm. He made a fist and hurled the powder toward the sky, which was suffused with white light.

Along with the infinity of bare branches resembling dried veins, his twig-like fingers pierced the blue sky, and a swirl of powder danced, borne on the wind. No new leaves sprouted, no blossoms bloomed.

But there was an instant proliferation of sounds. A swarm of sounds that might have been screams or laughter or war cries gnawed hungrily at each other's edges, filling the gaps between the trees and pouring in a murky foam from the little boy facing me, from his eyes and nose and mouth, where canines that hurt his lips danced like tiny flames.

THE CAKE SHOP IN
THE WOODS

Nothing I might encounter at the edge of the woods could surprise me anymore.

Once my son brought home a practically naked old woman with one breast exposed. She disappeared from his memory, leaving behind on the kitchen floor only a puddle of urine as cloudy as my confusion. Afterward, no matter how many times I asked, he insisted he didn't know any such old woman.

Another time, in the woods my son and I saw the swaying, swollen belly of a dead pregnant woman whom I took to be a refugee. Refugees were apparent not just on the big road going past our town but in the town itself, which is so small you might drive right by it and never notice. Other refugees were said to be hiding in the woods, though whether it was true or not I don't know. Right around then, I had discovered my son was sneaking food from the house and taking it into the woods. I didn't think he was giving it to refugees, though, because when he saw the pregnant woman lying dead in the woods, he cried and ran away.

All I had to do was think about the woods and the sound would be there, stuck in my ears. And since we lived in a little house at the edge of the woods, I was unable to shove the woods outside of or into the depths of my consciousness. At first it was the sound of coughing—the sound a person makes while being strangled. That's what I thought it was. Even after I realized that the continual coughing was coming from me—my mind distressed, trying to escape a rising heaviness within—the sound from the woods never went away. Then it changed shape, either to put my mind at ease or simply to fool me. Now, rather than coughing, the woods rang with the sound of laughter insinuating itself into a twisted tree branch or trunk. To be certain that this sound wasn't also coming from me, as I was cooking or cleaning or reading a book—in short, no matter what I was doing—I would gaze out the window. I saw laughter torn by the north wind turn into a vine with leaves like broken glass and a stem like barbed wire that wrapped itself around the trees in the woods. Its embrace must have been painful, for the trees contorted their branches and trunks as if in agony and began to drop their leaves. With the trees stripped bare, the view opened up, and my gaze would have thrust deeper into the woods had not my terror of encountering a withering gaze in return made me look away.

Before the winter turned bitter, the three of us—or, rather, four, counting the unborn child my wife was carrying—went for walks in the woods when cold air would curl up to our skin as if trying to warm itself, biting with its snaggleteeth. Several times I invited my son to go for a walk with me, but he always cried and protested. I guess he didn't want to go unless his mother came too. The days grew yet colder, and we didn't go into the woods much at all.

As the soon-to-be-born baby's birthday drew near, we decided to buy a cake.

A birthday for someone not born yet?

So we decided to designate my wife's birthday for the soon-to-be-born baby girl's.

The idea to make her birthday the same as her mother's could have come from either me or my son. It worked out well for both of us. If I'd said it was Mommy's birthday, he'd have been dragged back to the reality that she wasn't there and start to cry again. For a void to exist, a place in reality needs to have been occupied. Territory in another's memory must be secured for your presence to be remembered. Of course my son knew that his little sister existed—to the degree that she responded to his voice from within her mother's womb—but his memory of that dark, warm fluid in which he himself had once floated wasn't strong enough for him to grasp her existence as reality.

I don't know whether the dwarfs we saw were refugees living hidden in the woods or, as local legend had it, mischievous imps that ventured out of the woods to interfere in human affairs.

Light slowly filled the window, as if someone had tipped over a big jar of morning. Leaves lying flattened on the ground, having borne the weight of the night—which grew longer and heavier each day—were now pierced by millions of needles that the sun showered down. As the air lifted lightly in wind or turned itself vigorously inside out, silver thread firmly sewed up every seam. Nothing, therefore, could move. Yet squinting into the dazzle, I thought I could see time, having lost sight of landmarks to rely on, going back and forth over the brown carpet of earth between the woods and our house. Then, out of that static landscape came the sound of someone treading on dried leaves—an irregular sound, more suggestive of stirring or mixing than walking—and although the sound drew closer, I could see nothing, so I thought my sense of not only time but also distance must be off. Was the source of this confusion in the exterior world or in me? I tried not to think about it. The fallen leaves scraped against each other, giving off such heat that the dry air seemed about to ignite. My breathing came with difficulty, as if the house were already in flames.

Unable to bear this tension, I opened the kitchen door, and there at a point midway between the woods and the house, not wrapped in flames but giving off clouds of steam, stood a pair of dwarfs.

Their bodies were pressed closely together, shoulder to shoulder, one facing me and the other with his back to me, and yet I had the peculiar impression that a single individual was simultaneously showing me his front and his back. The dry leaves rustled with a noise like a giggle, and the two bodies made a half-turn with their contact as the axis. The one that had been showing his back turned frontward, and the one that had been facing me now had his back turned my way. But nothing changed. They made another half-turn, then another. Was the scene repeating itself because time had stagnated, or were the dwarfs causing time to stagnate?

The dwarfs' movements could also, I supposed, have shown hesitation over whether to return to the woods or come to our house. I was stumped.

But one thing I knew: they were not threatening. Usually when you meet someone, their back isn't visible. Seeing someone you know from behind, you think with surprise, *Is* that *what he looks like?* Or on seeing someone from behind and thinking it's someone you know, you run after them, only to discover on seeing their face that it's a total stranger. Perhaps this is the uncertainty, the precariousness, of human identity. My question as to whether I was seeing two dwarfs or a single (likely male) dwarf showing me his front and back simultaneously required no answer. By simultaneously showing back and front, that is, by presenting a complete picture of themselves, the dwarfs–since I saw two figures I will use the plural–probably wanted to demonstrate that their existence entailed no discrepancies, nothing hidden or malign, but only an unblemished consistency. They were two, yet indisputably one. As if in response, in order to show myself to them without concealment, I found myself spinning around and around in the kitchen doorway.

They used the language of this country. Perhaps their big heads with protuberant foreheads—for some reason I thought of Edgar Allan Poe as portrayed by Baudelaire—made it hard for them to keep their balance, for they stuck close together, supporting each other and spinning around as they drew near, always in the same posture, but not in a straight path, veering first one way and then another. Even more than their steps, which resembled the path taken by a drunken whirlwind, their speech was halting, twisted, peculiar. It was no ordinary way of talking, or none that I had ever encountered, but was that because it wasn't my native tongue? Or did it have to do with a mental or physical impairment of theirs? I didn't have the proficiency to judge.

They did talk a lot. I cannot transcribe what they said. It would be false of me even to try, for to be honest, there was a lot I couldn't catch. My linguistic ability was suddenly wanting.

After the dwarfs left, the kitchen floor was littered with their words, which were indistinguishable from dry and withered leaves riddled with wormholes. I picked up a handful and arranged them in a row on the floor. Should they be read from the left or the right? Maybe they were meant to be vertical. And were they in the right order, were there no missing letters? I had no idea. I became a scholar, hoping to decipher lost writings of ancient times:

now bringing my face up close to the lined-up leaves, now rearing back, now squinting through one eye and deliberately letting my gaze go out of focus. My son found this amusing, and obliged me by laughing. His body swayed happily as he imitated my movements in front of the lined-up leaves.

"Those guys must have wanted to say something. What do you think it was?" I asked him.

"That's right," he said, reverting to the style of speech of more infantile days when, despite not knowing what we meant when we spoke to him, he would respond with unfailing sociability. He looked up at me and tilted his head.

I laughed, scooped up dead leaves in both hands, and threw them out the kitchen door into the backyard. In response to my gesture, a strong wind came up and another cluster of leaves swished past my feet into the kitchen. Even after I shut the door, the leaves continued to rustle for a while, scurrying restlessly like insects.

"Lookit."

My son crouched down, gingerly reached out to touch the leaf-insects, and grabbed onto something. The withered leaves, as if determined not to be deprived of half-eaten food, grasped his fingers. Frightened, he let go with a jerk and fell back on his bottom.

The leaves surrounded him, but I kicked and scattered them away.

"It's okay," I told him.

A scrap of paper was left on the floor. I picked it up.

"Show me." He clung to me like a leaf and tugged on my pants. "Show me."

I kneeled down and showed him the scrap of paper. It was old and yellowed, and the words scribbled on it were badly smeared; someone had touched them with a wet hand. Even so, I could make out what was written.

"Show me! Show me! Show me!"

I laughed. "Here, take a good look. Can't you see it?"

"What is it?" He looked at me, fear and curiosity in his eyes.

How typical of a child, to become so excited he couldn't see what was in front of his nose.

He had acquired the ability to read, albeit haltingly, the words of picture books in his mother tongue, but he couldn't read the local language. He must have been further rebuffed by the distinctive handwriting.

"It's the name and address of a cake store," I explained.

"A cake store," he repeated, his eyes shining.

"So that was it," I said to myself. "They came to tell us this."

When I invited my son along to buy the birthday cake, I wasn't thinking about the cake store written on the scrap of paper but the shopping center across town where a big, warehouse-like supermarket had a kiosk that sold baked goods.

In front of this kiosk was a bench where my son could

have sat while he ate whatever treat I'd bought for him. Instead, for no clear reason, I never wanted to linger. SUMMER ONLY! said a sign tacked on the wall, but soft-serve ice cream was available year-round, and it was what my son always wanted. Holding his cone in two hands, he would soon be sporting a thick white mustache that'd grow longer and thicker as I urged him out to the parking lot, even as he kept turning around to look at the bench. The bench had gotten into his mind. He would soon enough be distracted, but every time we went to the shopping center, he was drawn to the bench, which seemed to summon some memory of his and was always there, never disappearing.

But I didn't think he had any memory of the cake store at the edge of the woods. We used to go there before he was born. My wife found it on one of our walks. She was ambling along next to me when she saw something in the distance, and then she pointed and cried out, "Look!"

Between the billows of green landscape scattering silver light, the spire of a church tower thrust into a low-hanging cloud, spilling sunlight onto a little village in the valley. Along the road leading to the church square stretched a row of houses built in the traditional style of the region. Timber frames stood out like sinew against light-gray stone walls. The houses seemed enveloped in a distant time, patiently awaiting the advent of something.

We entered the village out of sheer curiosity, but I was immediately struck by a sense of familiarity. Does this ever happen in a land utterly unlike where one was born and grew up?

"If we were going to live at the edge of the woods," I murmured, "a town like this would be nice."

My wife, who was walking ahead of me, turned around. "Actually," she said, "you only feel that way because you know there's no chance you'll ever live here."

She was heading toward the line of cars parked along the road and stopped next to one particular car, gritty like all the others from exposure to the elements. Somehow this fit in with the age-old landscape where everything seemed to have been in place for centuries, a witness to time passing by. Seeing my wife standing in that tableau caused me to catch my breath. She hesitated, and then with a click, she swung the car door open.

"See there?" she said, looking triumphantly at the driver's seat.

"Goodness," I said. "The key's in the ignition." And like the timid soul I am, I looked around to see if anybody was watching.

"It means get the hell out," said my wife.

I yawped in surprise. The look on my face must have been priceless, because she started to crack up.

"Get out?" I said. "Us? We're supposed to get out?"

"That's right," she said, after she'd finally stopped laughing. But mirth still bubbled in her eyes. "They want us to get in this car and get the hell out of here."

"Who does?"

"Hmm." She tilted her head merrily.

"So we're personae non gratae?"

"Hmm." She tilted her head again. "Shall I ask?"

I laughed again, but she'd already stepped away from the car and was in front of the cake shop, about to go inside. Next thing I knew, she was standing before the glass display case.

Bakeries in these parts generally sell cakes and pastries as well as bread. But the lettering on the shop window indicated that this place sold pastries and nothing else.

At the time, we hadn't yet begun venturing deep into the woods, but only walked timidly on the path around it.

Why were we hesitant to step into the woods? It might have been the stories we'd heard from the farmer and his wife, our landlords, and from other villagers about the imps who lived in the woods and stole children before they were born. The villagers related these stories laughingly when they learned we had no children. When we frowned at the idea—steal an unborn child from its mother's womb? How?—they held up their thumb and index finger a small distance apart. I guessed this meant that an imp was tiny enough to sneak in and steal an embryo. But then a villager started gesturing, making the shape of a swollen belly and, with two hands, demonstrating the size of a newborn baby, then waving a hand in front of his face to indicate "no good." This I took to mean that a grown fetus was too big for an imp to steal.

After that little exchange, I couldn't shake the worry that imps lurked in the dim corners of our bedroom, spying on us. Apparently neither could my wife.

"We can't give the imps an opening," she'd whisper in my ear, laughing as if something tickled. And so, leaving no space between our two bodies to make sure any embryo wouldn't be stolen, we pressed ourselves more closely together than we ever had. We owe our son's birth to the imps, you might say.

When my wife's pregnancy became evident—by which time my conversational ability had become passable, though with a heavy accent—the villagers told us we should still beware of imps encroaching from the woods. They said this with a vague smile, so we couldn't be sure if they were serious or joking.

Not too long after that, my wife went back to stay with her parents. She'd miscarried once before and wasn't taking any chances.

After she left, I stopped going to the pastry shop, partly because I've never had much of a sweet tooth. But then I began going for walks in the woods, and on one occasion I took it in my head to go back to the shop.

The village was still there. When I stepped into it, though, something felt different. In appearance it was almost exactly like others near the woods, but I was sure I hadn't wandered by mistake into the wrong village. I suspect the cause of the sense of a difference lay in me.

The pastry shop was still there, too. But it was closed;

perhaps the mother and daughter were on their lunch break.

The shop had a plate-glass front, yet the interior was strangely dark. My wife leaned over to look at the pastries in the display case, appearing not to notice the woman watching us from the kitchen.

There were rhubarb tarts and apricot tarts, which looked very tasty, but the flies flitting around inside the case disturbed me. Not a good sign. Flies are undiscriminating when it comes to nourishment—the sweet-sour juice of rhubarb and body fluid leaking from a wound are the same to them.

My wife looked up and greeted the woman with no sign of surprise.

"That's all we have again today," the woman said without a glance at the case.

Again today?

"No apple tarts?" asked my wife.

"Not the season for them," said the woman.

"Oh, right." My wife turned to me, stuck out her tongue, and shrugged.

"But the season hasn't got anything to do with it, does it?" said a voice. It was mine. My wife signaled me with her eyes, trying to get me to stop, but I paid no attention to her and went right on making needless remarks. I even laughed sardonically. "You always have only these for sale, don't you?"

I didn't mean that yesterday, today, and tomorrow they offered nothing but the same kind of tarts. What I really meant was: Yesterday, today, and tomorrow you offer nothing but these exact same tarts for sale, isn't that so? Inedible, fake plastic replicas of tarts that have no sell-by dates. But wait, what about those flies flitting from one tart to the next? Were they insane enough to think the plastic tarts were real?

The woman didn't reply. Behind her there was a quickening of the darkness, and out stepped a great lump of white flesh, so white it was translucent, the flesh seemingly held together by an irregular mesh of blood vessels that might burst at any moment. I stared, as the skin was imbued with darkness, deepening in color and tone. Along with the weakening oscillations of the atmosphere, my breath at last calmed, as did the mound of flesh before me.

Mff, mff, mff. With the sounds of muffled sighing, the air grew thick, gelatinous. This was a truly large girl. It seemed incongruous that she could have emerged from behind the slight old woman (that's how it had appeared to me). She was easily a head taller, but her bulk did not seem real. Her shiny chestnut hair, cut straight across her forehead, looked like a helmet. Yet, despite her gigantic physique, she seemed fragile, vulnerable, steeped in infancy, helpless. Her corpulence might suggest suffocation, but one swipe by something violent could erase her existence.

Although the woman and the large girl looked nothing alike, I saw that they were mother and daughter. In the woman's gaze, fixed on the girl with a vague sadness, and the girl's way of heedlessly expanding her own existence at her mother's side, one could clearly sense the ties woven between them.

"I think I'll have the apricot tart," said my wife's voice.

The woman nodded silently, picked up a knife, and opened the display case. The flies flew off in a frenzy, drawing characters in the air that disappeared as soon as they were formed, like incantations of a devil.

"That's plenty, thank you," my wife said.

The woman didn't do a very clean job of it, crushing the fruit so that thick juice ran. She used the knife as a spatula and laid the quarter-tart slice in a paper box. In a flash, a hand reached out from behind her, and the girl grabbed the slice of tart and stuffed it into her mouth. As she chewed the tart, then licked her fingers, her expression did not change. For a moment, it looked as if she were scraping flesh from her fingers and eating it.

I was afraid, thinking that the mother would yell at the daughter. I couldn't take my eyes off the knife in the woman's hand.

"Looks yummy," said my wife's voice.

I stared at her.

"Doesn't it?" She tilted her head and looked at me. I'd seen the same gesture somewhere before.

I remember thinking she reminded me of someone.

Afterward it seemed impossible. The thing is, that gesture was one that our son, who wasn't born yet, would make as he got older. *He* resembles *her*. There's no way she could have resembled him back when he might not even have been conceived.

I was often captivated by the way my son's expressions and movements, even simply his air, would reveal things transmitted from his mother with her milk and warmth and first words. His mannerisms certainly. Sometimes I would be shaken, sensing her presence more strongly in his gestures than when she herself was beside me. Perhaps the smallness of a child's body meant that in the reflux between mother and child, the essential things are highly concentrated.

Sometimes I would see myself in my son in ways that filled me with consternation. If this goes on, my presence will accumulate like sediment in him, I would worry, afraid that my wife's presence would be covered over and cease to blossom. To maintain her presence intact inside him, I could no longer be with him. Yet if I weren't with him, I'd be unable to see my wife in a form so much more like her real self than the wife I knew. In either case, I'd never be able to really see her again.

The woman in the pastry shop looked at us over the counter. She wasn't smiling, but neither did she seem to be on the verge of tears. *Mff mff mff* was the only sound between us. The large girl's body retreated and was reabsorbed into the darkness. The air grew heavy and sticky, like dough, which someone in the kitchen had to be mixing and rolling out. *Mff mff mff.*

I can't remember what we bought that day or whether we left without buying anything. I think that I went back there several times since, but those memories, too, have become doubtful. It's possible that it was a single event, mixed and rolled out over and over. But not being a pastry chef or skilled at baking, I know nothing of texture, moistness, and viscosity. I simply go on working the dough. I don't know what to do with it. What should I make, and how?

After struggling with the dough, I gave up. I had thought to make use of the apples from our yard to make a pie. I used to watch my wife when she did it. I'd peel the apples while listening to music on the radio. But just because I used to watch her go through the steps didn't mean I knew how to do it. So why did I try? I knew a tarte tatin was way beyond my abilities, but naively I imagined making an ordinary apple pie was simple.

"Want to play with this?" I said to my son.

The pie dough was crumbly, but he was happy because he could do with it whatever he wanted. It was now poor-quality Play-Doh and I had no intention of asking him what he was making.

When he tired of the dough, we gathered up the scraps and scattered them in the backyard. He crowed with anticipation. However, as neither the birds nor of course the dwarfs came by, his excitement soon cooled. There was a mound of apples in the kitchen. The old tree had chosen now of all times to bear fruit, the way a person might emit sighs. They'd been pecked over by thrushes and eaten by worms, so they couldn't sit around long. They would spoil quickly. But the two of us couldn't possibly eat so many. Would we end up tossing them in the yard, too?

"Oww!" An apple my son threw had hit one of the dwarfs smack on his forehead, making him cry out, so that the dwarf's other half couldn't help rubbing his own bumpy forehead in turn, making my son chortle. Couldn't something like that happen?

"Shall we go?"

I put my son in the car.

The supermarket in the shopping center wasn't very crowded. It'd been a while since I'd taken him to the bakery there. Usually I picked times when there was a TV show on that he wanted to watch and went shopping by myself.

"Which one do you want?" I asked.

"These," he said, pointing.

The display case of transparent plastic was jammed with gummy candies of all colors and shapes. I smiled.

"We came here for a birthday cake, you know."

"These, these." He looked like he might cry.

"We'll get some of those, too," I said, and asked for a big cake loaded with strawberries. My son looked at me as if he might burst into tears at any moment. I felt like teasing him: *Your face looks like a pastry that didn't come out right.* But it was at times like this that his face was a dead ringer for my ugly mug. "Okay, okay."

While I paid, he took off ahead of me, clutching the bag of gummies.

"Hey, wait."

He stopped in surprise and looked back at me. Pointing, he said, "I'm gonna share."

"Share?"

He nodded and ran off.

I knew where he was going.

But the usual people weren't on the bench.

Whenever I came shopping, no matter the time of day, a mother and her little girl would be there. Invariably they wore the same clothing. Without their uttering a word, I knew they weren't from this country. In terms of being outsiders, we were perhaps the same. And yet there are outsiders and then there are *outsiders*. There's a world of difference between a person who's truly treated like an outsider and a person with a place to live, somewhere to go home to, peering into the mirror and—as if finding a blemish or a liver spot—asking themselves, *Am I an outsider?* I was at least able to look into the mirror that way, but not everyone even has a mirror. Every time I saw the mother and daughter on the bench, time stopped. Shut inside time, all I could do was stand by as everything repeated itself—I was forced to wait.

The mother did not relax but leaned forward, chin in hand, staring down with unfocused eyes. The little girl chattered away. At times a smile would come to the mother's lips, only to be wiped away by a look of exhaustion. The girl's sweet laughter was like spangles of light but didn't last long, sensitive as she was to the pain overwhelming her mother. Anxiety had kneaded the mother's existence into a tenuous form, even as it absorbed the girl's laughter and created the mass of mother and child. But what could keep that mass from crumbling? In the girl's eyes there was the sense that even if the mass crumbled, if in the crumbled bits she and her mother were mingled, then she wouldn't mind. And although a force within her might make her want to roam, she resisted, holding herself back from that impulse, never straying far from her mother's side. When her mother's gaze wandered, the girl would draw close and wrap her mother's slackened gaze around her again like a lifeline.

Were the mother and daughter really not there? Or was I afraid to have my own helplessness impressed upon me? Was I frightened of being a mere observer? If out of my sight, were they gone? Could I have forgotten them?

My son watched. And he could hear his mother's voice. When she found him hiding a bag of treats from a friend, especially someone smaller than him, she always said, "Share." He remembered. "You're going to be a big brother now." He knew. He was ready to share. To hold out a hand. Just as all his life he'd held out his small hand in response to hands held out to him.

And with keen sensitivity he had picked up on the wretched helplessness given off by his father. So if he did want to share, it was with that mother and daughter–and with me. I was preventing him from responding to the impulse that propelled him. But he could do nothing. The mother and daughter were gone.

The person there now was a sixtyish woman resting beside her purchases. The spot where the little girl always skittered around was occupied by white plastic bags full of groceries.

"Time to go," I said.

I took him by the hand and led him away. He turned to look back, again and again.

When we got home, after we took the cake out of its box, my son started bawling. He'd been quiet, a bit downcast, in the car ride home. Now he had tears rolling down his face. What was wrong? Don't drive me crazy, kid. I was ready to start weeping myself. If he started crying for his mother, there'd be nothing I could do.

"Tell me what's wrong," I said. "I haven't got a clue."

After a while he finally stopped crying. He puffed out his cheeks and then blew out his breath. Finally I understood.

I'd slipped up. It was a birthday cake, but I'd forgotten to get candles. I had a vague memory of the clerk asking me if I needed candles, but I couldn't remember answering.

"Sorry. Bad Daddy."

I asked if he wanted to go back to the shopping center for candles with me, but he said he wanted to watch TV. It was time for his favorite Claymation program. *Well, you never want to miss something like that, do you*, I thought, chagrined but relieved.

It was starting to get dark out, and as I neared the shopping center, I had to switch on the headlights. Suddenly I began to worry if it was wrong to have left my son home alone. I had locked the door, but would he open it to invite the old woman with one breast exposed in again? Or the dwarfs?

I imagined the dwarfs plopped on the sofa with my son between them, all three with eyes glued to the TV screen. On the show were characters (human? animal?) that looked exactly like the dwarfs; the surfaces of their bodies would develop lumps that moved as if bugs were rampaging under the skin. While they watched this, the dwarfs might press hard on their foreheads, which would be undergoing crustal change. My son wouldn't notice. On screen, the characters would open their eyes as if raising window shades, open their mouths as if unlocking drawers, and utter words as if throwing out rotten apples or dead beetles. Just where the body-shaking laughter and sighs and cries of astonishment were coming from, neither my son nor the dwarfs cuddled against him, eyes on the TV, would know. After a time, just as on the screen, the dwarfs' foreheads would split open with a dramatic noise.

Feeling something sopping wet, thick, and soupy fly onto his cheeks from either side, my son would look to the left and right, but he'd be alone in the dark room. Crushed by loneliness, he would be seeking the security of the most important person to him...

I was desperate to get home. There were few customers in the bakery, no line of people waiting to buy bread. Even so, it took time. I wasn't sure if the woman behind the counter was the same as the one before or not. She had eyes like a grazing cow, and stared at me as I repeated the words: *Candles for a birthday cake*. In the middle of my third or fourth try, she turned unsteadily and waddled into the back. She seemed unaware that she'd dropped her white cap, unaware that she'd trampled it. I wasn't sure if she'd even understood what I'd said. What was taking so goddamn long? All she had to do was go get me some frigging candles. Frustrated, I leaned over the counter and peered into the back of the store.

It was dimly lit. I pictured the woman in the pastry shop at the edge of the woods. She was flailing her arms, struggling to keep from hitting her daughter. The large girl's body was bent over. All around her was a darkness, red from the heat of the oven, that trembled slightly. I heard a voice. Whether it was scolding or lamenting, I couldn't tell.

From afar I could see the light in the kitchen. When I got out of the car, dry leaves came up to me, playful as puppies. I paused to peer quietly into the kitchen through the window.

In the center of the table, just where I'd left it, was the birthday cake box. Four places were set around it. None of them were for the dwarfs. Next to my son's plate, which had Babar the Elephant on it, was the one he had designated as Mommy's–it had a design of strawberries and was not to be used by anyone else.

Had the dwarfs gone back into the woods? I could hear merry laughter coming from the living room.

I brought out a platter from the cupboard and set the cake on it. I emptied out the little paper bag containing the candles from the shopping center bakery.

Now I saw why it had taken the woman in the bakery so long to accomplish that simple task. The six little birthday candles that fell out of the bag were each a different color. That cow-eyed woman had wanted in her own way to bring joy to a small child. She'd bent her outsized body over and carefully chosen each one.

There were a few too many for his age. No matter. "White, red, pink, blue, yellow, green." Pronouncing the name of each color carefully, the way my wife did when she was teaching him, I stuck the candles among the ruby red strawberries dotting the top of the cake.